PLAN OF ACTION

LANTERN BEACH PD, BOOK 5

CHRISTY BARRITT

River Heights

COMPLETE BOOK LIST

Squeaky Clean Mysteries:

#13 Cold Case: Clean Getaway

#14 Cold Case: Clean Sweep

While You Were Sweeping, A Riley Thomas Spinoff

The Sierra Files:

#1 Pounced

#2 Hunted

#3 Pranced

#4 Rattled

#5 Caged (coming soon)

The Gabby St. Claire Diaries (a Tween Mystery series):

The Curtain Call Caper

The Disappearing Dog Dilemma

The Bungled Bike Burglaries

The Worst Detective Ever

#1 Ready to Fumble

#2 Reign of Error

#3 Safety in Blunders

#4 Join the Flub

#5 Blooper Freak

#6 Flaw Abiding Citizen

#7 Gaffe Out Loud

#8 Joke and Dagger (coming soon)

Raven Remington

Relentless 1

Relentless 2 (coming soon)

Holly Anna Paladin Mysteries:

#1 Random Acts of Murder

#2 Random Acts of Deceit

#2.5 Random Acts of Scrooge

#3 Random Acts of Malice

#4 Random Acts of Greed

#5 Random Acts of Fraud

#6 Random Acts of Outrage

#7 Random Acts of Iniquity (coming soon)

Lantern Beach Mysteries

#1 Hidden Currents

#2 Flood Watch

#3 Storm Surge

#4 Dangerous Waters

#5 Perilous Riptide

#6 Deadly Undertow

Lantern Beach Romantic Suspense

Tides of Deception

Shadow of Intrigue

Storm of Doubt

Lantern Beach P.D.

On the Lookout

Attempt to Locate

First Degree Murder

Dead on Arrival

Plan of Action (coming in May)

Carolina Moon Series

Home Before Dark

Gone By Dark

Wait Until Dark

Light the Dark

Taken By Dark

Suburban Sleuth Mysteries:

Death of the Couch Potato's Wife

Fog Lake Suspense:

Edge of Peril

Margin of Error (coming soon)

Cape Thomas Series:

Dubiosity

Disillusioned

Distorted

Standalone Romantic Mystery:

The Good Girl

Suspense:

Imperfect

The Wrecking

Standalone Romantic-Suspense:

Keeping Guard

The Last Target

Race Against Time

Ricochet

Key Witness

Lifeline

High-Stakes Holiday Reunion

Desperate Measures

Hidden Agenda

Mountain Hideaway

Dark Harbor

Shadow of Suspicion

The Baby Assignment

The Cradle Conspiracy (coming soon)

Nonfiction:

Characters in the Kitchen

Changed: True Stories of Finding God through Christian Music (out of print)

The Novel in Me: The Beginner's Guide to Writing and Publishing a Novel (out of print)

PROLOGUE

MORIAH GILEAD HELD her breath as she watched the figure descend the steps into the dark, cave-like bunker. She blinked, the glaring daylight behind the man preventing her from seeing any of his features.

She and her friend Serena stood side by side, gripping each other's arms. Neither of them seemed to be breathing. Only dreading. Waiting. Fearing.

The man took a few more steps and paused in front of them. Moriah's vision cleared, but she still wasn't sure who the man was.

Not Gilead. Gilead was taller. More imposing. He walked with a swagger.

He almost looked like . . .

"Dietrich . . ." Serena muttered.

Yes, Dietrich. It *was* Dietrich. The man was one of

Gilead's right-hand men. Was he down here to punish them or to help?

Moriah would guess based on his glare and stiff motions that he was here to *punish* them.

"What are you doing, Serena?" Dietrich asked.

"I was worried about Moriah," she rushed, still gripping Moriah's arm. "I saw those men bringing her here, and I knew something was wrong. So I came here to check on her."

"It's not your business to interfere in Gilead's marriage." Dietrich sounded as staunch as his stance in front of them.

Serena continued to squeeze Moriah's arm tighter —tight enough that it hurt. Moriah hardly noticed. Instead she held her breath, waiting to see what would happen next.

Freedom had felt so close, if even just for a moment.

"I'm hardly interfering in a marriage," Serena said, her voice wobbly. "I'm helping to save a life."

Dietrich remained stoic, seemingly unaffected by Serena's words. "You need to go."

"Not without Moriah." Serena's squeeze became a death grip.

"Moriah isn't going anywhere."

As Dietrich said the words, the pit in Moriah's stomach deepened. She wouldn't be rescued, would she? Instead, her husband was going to keep her chained in this black abyss, a place straight from her nightmares.

Gilead would probably do enough to keep her alive—but barely. She'd either suffer a long death or beg for mercy until Gilead allowed her to return to the compound, under the condition that she act as his robot for the rest of her life. Even then, if she ever messed up, she'd be punished again and again and again.

There would be no happy ending for her. She felt certain.

The thought caused a swell of panic to rise in her. Something nearly inhuman sprouted to life inside of Moriah. A guttural sound escaped from the depths of her soul, and she charged toward the daylight.

"No!" she shouted.

Before she made it to the first step, hands gripped around her waist and jerked her back, preventing her from reaching the precious freedom just ahead of her.

Dietrich. He'd grabbed Moriah, his lithe body stronger than she'd anticipated.

"Stop it, Moriah," he growled in her ear. "You're only going to make things worse."

She had no intention of stopping. Instead, she thrashed in his arms, clawing at his skin, and kicking back at his legs without mercy.

"Get off her!" Serena yelled.

He moaned and paused. Based on Dietrich's movements, Moriah would guess that Serena had leapt onto his back.

They fought him from both sides.

A surge of hope sprang to life inside Moriah. Together they could take him down. Surely . . .

Moriah heard an *umph* as something slammed into the ground, then a grunt.

She sucked in a quick breath.

Serena?

The brief moment of distraction gave Dietrich the opportunity to shove Moriah away. As she hit the wall, the air whooshed from her lungs. A dull ache started in her head.

She moaned and let her head fall to the side. That's when she saw Serena. Her friend lay on the floor, holding her wrist, with her face twisted in pain.

Dietrich stared at both of them, his breaths coming quickly. His nostrils flared. His hands were clenched at his side.

"If you two would just listen, we wouldn't have any of these problems," he growled.

"Dietrich, you're a good man," Serena pleaded, scooting away from him as survival instincts seemed to take over. She still rubbed her wrist. Had she broken it? "You've got to help us."

His gaze darkened. "You're right. I am a good man. I'm obeying orders, just like I should."

"You know you can't listen to Gilead," Moriah continued. "He's losing his mind."

"He's very upset right now. The election was ruled invalid, and he has to do all of this again. We were so close to victory." Dietrich frowned and shook his head. "I don't know why I'm telling you this. You don't even care about the Cause. You never did, did you?"

"Dietrich, it's not right to make people suffer," Serena said. "You know that."

Moriah watched the conversation. Serena obviously had feelings for this man, and she could see why. Dietrich was handsome and smart and loyal.

But he'd been brainwashed by Anthony Gilead, just like everyone else here.

Moriah had little hope they'd be able to get through to him. After all, in the weeks since she'd been here, no one from the outside world had been able to reach Moriah. But she hadn't faced the truth of this precarious situation until she'd realized her life was on the line. If only she'd taken that police chief up on her offer to help, Moriah might not be in this condition right now.

"It's hard sometimes to realize that our disobedience will have consequences," Dietrich said, his glare sliding between the two of them. "I had to learn the hard way as well."

"Did Gilead send you here?" Moriah's voice cracked, sounding as hollow as the space around her.

"No, he doesn't know that I came."

"Then don't tell him," Moriah pleaded. "Don't tell him any of this happened. Let us go."

Maybe it wasn't too late to fix this situation. Moriah could hope, at least.

Dietrich shook his head and let out a frustrated chuckle. "Don't you realize everything he has riding on you, Moriah? You need to be by his side when the polls open again next week for the election. But he can't risk you pulling any stunts and ruining what he's worked so hard to build. That's why he has to do things this way. It's for your own good."

"There are better ways," Serena said, still imploring him, with desperation in her eyes. "This is pure evil, Dietrich. If you look deep down in yourself, you'd realize that. People shouldn't be treated this way. Chained in a dark bunker against her will when her only crime was disobeying her husband."

"It's not evil!" His voice sliced through the air. "It's discipline. And there's nothing wrong with it."

Silence stretched across the space as reality settled over Moriah. They couldn't talk themselves out of this situation. They were in too deep.

Dietrich might as well be a diehard Nazi following after Hitler. He'd been brainwashed to the extent there was no changing his mind.

"What are you going to do with us?" Serena asked.

"I need to report back to Gilead," he finally said.

Tears sprang to Moriah's eyes as she considered the consequences. Each possibility was sure to bring her pain. "You don't have to do that. We won't tell anyone you were a part of this. Just let us go."

His jaw twitched. "I can't do that."

"You can do it, Dietrich," Serena said softly. "You know you can. I know you're a good person. I saw you feeding that feral cat with your leftovers in the woods behind your house. I know you carry a picture of your mother in your Bible. There's still an honorable man buried deep inside you, someone who cares about the world around him."

At once, Dietrich drew himself up and took a step back. "I can't help either of you. Now I've got to go. I should have never come here in the first place."

Serena lunged for him but missed, gasping with pain as her already injured wrist hit the ground. "Stop! Please! You can't leave us down here."

"I have no other choice."

"You always have a choice, Dietrich." Serena's voice took on an air of quiet desperation.

Her hopeless tone chilled Moriah far more than the sound of her panic did.

"Not this time." He stomped over to Serena, grabbed her uninjured arm, and fastened it to a cuff above her head. Then he did the same with Moriah.

With one last scowl at both of them, he plodded up the steps, and the door slammed, leaving Moriah and Serena in total darkness.

Moriah couldn't even look at Serena, the woman who'd come to rescue her. Instead, she gave in to the despair that had been fighting to claim her. Tears poured down her face.

She'd dug her own grave . . . and now she was going to die in it.

CHAPTER ONE

POLICE CHIEF CASSIDY CHAMBERS took a bite of her grilled cheese and peach sandwich, savoring the unusual flavor combination. She had to get back to work, but she wanted to enjoy the time with the gang for just a bit longer.

She and her friends had all gathered for an early lunch at The Crazy Chefette after an especially stressful couple of days here on Lantern Beach. The good news was that her friend Lisa Dillinger had finally been cleared in her supposed role in a food poisoning epidemic and the local mayoral election had been rescheduled, with the old results tossed out.

They had those two things to celebrate, at least. For a moment, Cassidy wouldn't dwell on all the worries that still wanted to creep into her mind like guests who'd outstayed their welcome. There was so much on the line right now. So much.

Cassidy finished her sandwich, tossed her plate in the trash, and moseyed over to her husband, Ty. He sat at the table, his head resting on a hand splayed across his forehead. He looked like his mind was a million miles away.

He wasn't acting like himself at all right now. It could be the effects of the food poisoning that had crippled many residents here. Whatever it was, Ty looked like he needed to lie down and escape from the world for a while.

Cassidy laid her hand on his arm and leaned closer. "You should go home."

He didn't argue—a sure sign he wasn't feeling well. Instead, he stood and walked with her to the edge of the room, away from an especially rowdy conversation about who was the best volleyball player in the group.

It was good that her friends' normal banter was returning. Everyone had been under too much stress lately. The events as of late had been like watching a storm destroy your island and knowing you could do nothing about it. All the residents here had felt it.

"I hate to admit it, but I think maybe you're

right," Ty said, his eyes dull and absent of their normal spark and intelligence.

"You hate to admit I'm right?" Cassidy teased, poking his abdomen.

"I hate to admit you're right about needing to leave." He sounded like he wanted to banter but couldn't. Instead, he flinched, and his hand went to his stomach.

Maybe she shouldn't be teasing him right now.

"I know, baby. I'm sorry you're not feeling well." Cassidy reached for the keys in her pocket. "I can drive you home."

Ty waved her off, but his face still looked pale and clammy. "No, I'll be fine. You get your work done at the office. I know you have a ton of administrative stuff to do. Then come home early. Maybe I'll feel better by then."

She squinted with concern. She'd be there for him in a heartbeat if he needed her. But it would be nice to knock out some paperwork, if possible. The crimes here on the island recently had resulted in nightmarish amounts of office hours.

"Are you sure? I don't mind taking you home and staying with you. I could even bring some of my files back to the house and—"

"I'll be fine, Cassidy." Ty lowered his hand from his abdomen and nodded, not quite selling his words. "I'd rather you not see me like this. I think if I get some rest, I'll be good to go."

"If you're sure." She knew that the former Navy SEAL needed, at times, to maintain a little of his macho tendencies, and she didn't want to push or baby him.

"I am." Ty kissed her cheek. "Good job on solving that last case, by the way. Everyone here on the island owes you their thanks."

"I'm just doing my job." She was simply happy to mark this case as done and to clear her friend's good name. Actually, not just one friend's good name—two friends.

"We all know it's more than a job to you." He stepped back and offered a slight wave, followed by a wink. "I'll call you later."

"Sounds good, hon. Love you."

Ty smiled. "Love you too, Cassidy."

Cassidy watched as he walked away, feeling a burst of love warm her insides. Ty was the man of her dreams, and though it had been a hard road to find each other, she wouldn't change a thing.

She hated the fact that he still felt ill. At least the person responsible for making everyone sick was now in custody. With the election rescheduled for one week from now, maybe Lantern Beach could finally get back on track.

When Ty was by her side, Cassidy felt as if she could conquer the world. She knew the island still had a lot of struggles—and they would until Anthony Gilead could be revealed for who he really was. But she couldn't wait until Ty was back to himself so they could face these problems together.

————

Ty's head swam as he headed down the road in his vintage Chevy truck, affectionately named Big Blue by his friends.

He hadn't let on to Cassidy just how bad he felt. His head hurt. Nausea roiled in his stomach. His body demanded rest, and he knew he couldn't remain upright for much longer.

Thankfully, his house wasn't far from The Crazy Chefette. He couldn't get there soon enough.

He gripped the steering wheel as he stared at the beautiful sky ahead. Lots of clouds rolled around high in the sky, and another darker line of storms lingered offshore, promising an interesting day weather-wise.

The past few days had passed like a blur.

He hadn't been able to stop thinking about what his friend Colton Locke had told him earlier. Apparently, during their last mission, as his SEAL team had rescued their target, there may have been another American at the terrorist compound. Had this other man been working for Akrum Abadi? Or had he been a captive forced into slavery there at the compound?

And what was this man's tie with Anthony Gilead? Could the man *be* Anthony Gilead?

The questions continued to gnaw at Ty.

One thing he knew for sure: it was no coincidence that Anthony Gilead had come to this island to start his little cult. He was somehow connected with Ty.

What Ty couldn't figure out was what this man's end game could possibly be. What he wanted. Why he was targeting Ty and Cassidy.

Ty was desperate to figure it out. But first he had to recover from this bout of food poisoning.

Just then, his phone rang. When he saw that it was Colton, he answered, putting it on speaker. "Hey, man. What's up?"

"I just heard something that I thought you might find interesting."

"What's that?" Ty glanced behind him and saw a black truck in his rearview mirror coming up on him fast.

Ty maintained his speed and waited for the vehicle to pass. Three seconds later, the driver was on his tail, nearly running him off the road in an attempt to get somewhere faster.

"What's your hurry?" Ty muttered, irritation pinching his muscles.

"What was that?" Colton asked.

"Nothing."

Ty glanced in the mirror again and saw the truck remained close—too close. Hopefully, the driver would pass instead of acting like a jerk. Didn't this guy know anything about living on island time? The briskness of city life was supposed to disappear once people arrived on Lantern Beach.

"Sorry about that," Ty turned back to his phone call. "Go ahead. What did you hear?"

"It's about Anthony Gilead."

Ty's pulse spiked at the mention of the man's name. "I'm all ears."

Before he could listen to what Colton had to say, the black truck's engine revved. The driver jerked into the other lane to pass Ty.

Finally.

Just as the truck with its dark-tinted windows pulled beside him, the driver veered into Ty's lane.

The vehicle collided with Ty's, hitting hard.

Ty swerved, but it was no use. Big Blue was out of his control.

He careened toward the massive ditch at the side

of the road. His front tires bumped off the pavement and continued going. Going. Going—

The right side of his truck collided with the side of the ditch.

Ty's body rammed into the steering wheel, and everything went black.

CHAPTER TWO

AS CASSIDY WALKED into the quiet lobby of the police station, she paused and had a moment of silence for all the changes that had happened here over the past year.

Former police chief Alan Bozeman had left, along with one of his officers.

Her receptionist was no longer here, and another officer had just resigned yesterday.

That left her and Dane . . . and she wasn't sure how Dane was feeling right now about working for her.

As if he'd been reading her mind, Officer Dane Bradshaw stepped from his office and offered a stiff nod. Cassidy sucked in a quick breath when she realized he'd come into work today. No one would blame him for taking time off after everything that had happened.

The man was in his mid-twenties, with dark hair cut short, and he'd just moved to this area from Cincinnati with his police dog, Ranger, a couple months ago.

"You're here." Cassidy paused in front of him in the small lobby, unable to ignore the tension that filled the air.

"I thought it would be good to keep my mind occupied," Dane said, still sounding rigid. "Otherwise, I'll just dwell on everything that happened. So I came into work."

"Probably smart. I appreciate it, especially now that Leggott turned in his resignation."

"I heard Braden is going to start."

Cassidy nodded. "That's right. But we're still going through some of the official paperwork. It's one of the things on my to-do list today."

Dane paused as the front desk phone rang. The call would go to Cassidy's phone in a moment—she was the one on duty. Instead, Dane picked up the line.

He mumbled a few things before nodding, hanging up, and stepping toward the door. "I'd stay and talk, but we just got a call about a truck in the ditch. Someone driving past reported it."

It wasn't entirely unusual here on Lantern Beach. Traffic incidents topped their workload during tourist season. "Any injuries?"

"The caller didn't say—just reported it. It's out not too far from your place. I'll call the rescue squad to meet me there, just in case."

Cassidy's shoulders tightened. A truck. Near her house.

Ty drove a truck.

"Is that right?" she asked, a subtle ache filling her throat. "Any other details?"

"No, the phone line was breaking up. Must have been one of those dead zones here on the island."

Making a split-second decision, Cassidy turned on her heel. "You know what? I think I'll go with you."

"I can probably handle this." Dane stared at her, as if trying to figure out if this was a slight against him or a reaction showing he hadn't regained Cassidy's trust.

"I know. But I'd like to go. Call it intuition. Or maybe I just don't want to stay inside the office. Either way, let's go check out what happened."

"Suit yourself." He flipped his keys around his finger.

Stepping outside, the bad feeling in Cassidy's gut grew—and she didn't even know why. It was like a sixth sense whispered to her that something was wrong, told her that she shouldn't stay at the office right now.

Hopefully, that sixth sense was wrong. Hopefully, this would be a fender bender with no injuries. Ty was probably at home in bed by now.

But Cassidy wouldn't relax until she knew for sure. Too much had gone wrong on this island lately.

She climbed in beside Dane, deciding to let him drive, and desperate to distract herself from the paranoia that reared in her mind. They headed down the area's main thoroughfare, a highway that stretched across the center of the narrow island.

Nearly fifty side streets branched out from this road, all leading to either the ocean or the Pamlico Sound. Homes, mostly vacation rentals, were sectioned off along those streets. The residences were starting to fill up as tourist season got closer and closer.

"Did you get any sleep last night?" Cassidy asked Dane over the wailing siren. Maybe she was just desperate to keep her mind occupied.

Her officer had just been released from his holding cell yesterday evening after he'd been set up to take the fall for another crime.

He shrugged. "A little. It just felt good to be back

at home with Ranger. Thanks for taking care of him for me."

"Kujo enjoyed the company." The two dogs had lain in the sand and barked at wayward birds during their time together, like two old friends catching up. Cassidy shifted. "Listen, I know I've already said this, but I'm really sorry about the way things played out."

"You were just doing your job and following the evidence. You had to prove I was set up before you could let me go. I understand."

Even as Dane said the words, Cassidy could hear the tautness in his voice. On a logical level, he understood what had happened. But on an emotional level, he sounded like he'd need some time to work through everything.

"By the way, someone stopped by with an application for the receptionist/dispatcher position this morning," Dane said, changing the subject without apology.

Cassidy blinked in surprise. "Really? That was fast."

"I guess this woman just came into town and was in the general store when people were talking about everything that went down. She decided to jump on the opportunity to try and snag a job. She seemed nice enough. I left the application on your desk."

"I'll check it out later." Cassidy stared ahead at the road. "Thanks."

The sky was bright blue and dotted with white clouds lined with gray. Forecasters were calling for a line of strong thunderstorms to come through starting this evening and lasting all day tomorrow, and a brisk wind seemed to tease at that.

"That must be the truck up there." Dane nodded straight ahead.

Cassidy's breath caught when she saw the rear end of the vehicle sticking out of one of the island's deeper ditches. She was still far away, but she was close enough to realize it was a blue truck.

A blue truck like the one Ty drove. Like Big Blue.

Her eyes froze on the scene, and she was unable to draw her gaze away.

Was that Ty's?

No, it couldn't be. Ty was a great driver. Always aware. Alert. Moving through life using all his Navy SEAL training and capabilities. The most reliable person she knew.

Besides, Ty would have called Cassidy in a situation like this.

Unless he was hurt and unable to do so.

Cassidy bit back a frown. Maybe she should have insisted on driving Ty home. He had looked awful when they'd been at The Crazy Chefette. What if Ty had a medical episode while in his truck and had crashed?

She reminded herself to stay rational. Getting worked up with "what ifs" would get her nowhere right now. She needed to keep a level head.

Her gaze scanned the street, but there were no other cars. "Did the caller not stay at the scene?"

Dane shrugged. "It doesn't look like it. He seemed to be in a hurry . . . I don't know."

As Dane drove closer, her heart thrummed in her ears even harder.

It was Ty's truck. Definitely.

Dane glanced at Cassidy as he pulled up behind it, a subtle intake of breath signaling he recognized the vehicle also. "Maybe you should wait here."

She hardly heard him. Instead, Cassidy climbed from the police cruiser and rushed toward the driver's side door. She prayed she wouldn't find Ty there, hurt and bent over the steering wheel. She prayed he was okay.

But when Cassidy reached the door, she saw that the vehicle was empty.

She glanced at Dane. Where had Ty gone? What was going on here?

———

Cassidy stared at the inside of Ty's truck. Blood spatter covered the steering wheel. His front window was shattered. His phone lay on the floor among broken shards of glass.

But Ty was gone.

Was he wandering around the island with a head injury? Was he having memory problems? Searching for help?

Her throat tightened at the thought, and a small gasp escaped.

"Chief?"

Dane's voice snapped her from her somber thoughts—for a moment, at least. She turned toward him and saw his concerned brown eyes studying her. "Yes?"

"What do you want to do?"

She tried to gather her thoughts, to figure out a plan of action. All she could think about was finding Ty. Emotion clouded her normal logic.

More sirens sounded in the distance. The ambulance was on its way. But there was no one here for EMTs to treat.

She had to think like an investigator. Like she would if she wasn't emotionally involved with this case. She needed to examine the scene. Look for evidence. Try to form a better picture of what had happened.

Cassidy stepped back from the truck. As she did, she saw the black scrape on the driver's door and sucked in a breath.

"Dane, this wasn't an accident. It looks like someone sideswiped him."

"And just left him?"

"Your guess is as good as mine." She swallowed the lump in her throat before squatting on the ground. Drops of blood splotched the blades of grass.

Carefully, she began following the trail. Across the grass. Toward the road. On the gravel.

She found two drops at the edge of the street.

And then there were none.

A surge of anxiety rushed through her. Drops of blood didn't just disappear.

Another vehicle had been here.

Just exactly what had happened on this road, less than a mile from her home?

Going back to Ty's truck, she carefully reached inside and grabbed his phone from the floor. The screen was busted. Just to be certain, she hit the power button.

Nothing happened. She wouldn't be getting clues from this device any time soon.

That meant she needed another plan, and there was only one thing that came to mind.

"I need you to process this scene and then have

Ty's truck towed back to the station," Cassidy told Dane. "I need to search for Ty. This accident just happened. He can't be but so far away."

Dane tossed her his keys. "Take my car. I'll be fine here for a while."

"Thanks." Without wasting any more time, Cassidy climbed back into the police cruiser. "And call Mac. Ask him to help—tell him to check my house, just in case Ty went there. We're going to need more eyes on this scene—as many as we can get."

"Where are you going?"

"If this was malicious, there's only one place I can think of where Ty might be. Gilead's Cove."

Alarm stretched across Dane's face. "Be careful, Chief. Ty wouldn't want you going there alone. You know how he feels about that place."

"I'll be careful." She didn't like the scenarios that wanted to play out in her mind, but nothing would stop her from searching for her husband. Nothing.

CHAPTER THREE

CASSIDY'S PULSE pounded furiously as she headed down the road. With each turn of the tires, her determination to find Ty grew.

Something bad had happened. Her husband was in danger. And she had to do something to help him.

On the short drive there, Cassidy had made a few calls. First, to the Coast Guard and then to the transportation system that operated the ferry. She'd also called down to the clinic to make sure that the man who'd called in the accident hadn't taken Ty in. The nurse at the front desk said she hadn't seen him but promised to call if she heard anything.

Why would the caller leave the scene like that?

Cassidy knew. Because the caller was the same person who'd run Ty off the road. This was a game, wasn't it?

She pressed hard on the brakes as she reached the gated entrance to Gilead's Cove. Dust flew up behind her tires. A small guard station sat there, huddled beside an iron fence that surrounded the entire property.

This place was once an RV park, but Anthony Gilead had bought the property less than a year ago. He claimed to be one of God's chosen ones. He said he'd found an undiscovered book of the Bible during a pilgrimage in the Middle East.

He had more followers than he should, but people were buying into what he was selling. Most of his members were poor, had suffered from addictions, had endured a lot of wounds in their lives. Gilead offered them room and board in return for their devotion—and, no doubt, their money.

Cassidy would guess there to be at least two hundred people here now.

Seeing no one in the guard station, she laid on her horn until a man appeared in the distance. He slowly trudged toward the gate, taking his precious time.

As sight of him became clearer, Cassidy realized she didn't recognize him from any of her earlier visits. He appeared to be in his late fifties and forty pounds overweight. As per standard garb for those who lived here, he wore a tunic and sandals.

The man climbed into the guard booth and

peered out, his sagging face displaying a mopey frown. He didn't seem surprised to see Cassidy. No, his expression remained level, maybe even bored.

"Can I help you, officer?" he asked.

"It's police chief. I need to get in. Now."

"I'll have to run that past—"

"I don't care what Anthony Gilead says. I need in."

His frown deepened. "As you know, I can't simply let you—"

She flashed her badge. "This badge says you can. This is a timely matter. Don't make me arrest you."

The man's face paled. To her surprise, he stopped arguing and pressed a button. A moment later, she heard a click, and the gate slowly swung open.

Cassidy pulled her car through, reminding herself not to drive too fast. There were children here, and she needed to be cautious, even though urgency rushed through her veins. Again, she reminded herself to control the impulses that reared their heads again and again.

She pulled to a stop in front of the Meeting Place, threw her car into Park, and strode inside the building. The Meeting Place was a central area here at the compound, one that used to serve as a community center back when this had been an RV park. Now members of Gilead's Cove ate here as well as engaged in some type of services or ceremonies where Anthony Gilead spoke and bestowed his so-called wisdom.

Everyone inside stopped what they were doing and turned to stare as the door slammed shut behind Cassidy. There were probably thirty people sitting at rows of tables, their heads silently bent over plates of food.

The building smelled like body odor and chicken noodle soup, and the air around her seemed one of oppression rather than freedom. Did everyone feel that here or was it just her?

Cassidy held up her badge again. "I'm looking for Anthony Gilead."

No one said anything.

She was about to put the pressure on when Gilead himself stepped down the staircase across the room, his eyes on her.

Cassidy's skin crawled at the sight of the man. His dark hair was perfectly coifed back from his face, he wore expensive-looking jeans and a button-up shirt that probably cost more than Cassidy made in a week.

What made it all worse was knowing that he got his money from unsuspecting followers who'd pledged Gilead their all.

"Cassidy, what can I do for you?" He sauntered

toward her, that arrogant swagger still present like always.

"I need to search your compound."

"Is everything okay?"

The saccharine concern in his voice only made her want to throttle the man. Cassidy leaned closer, barely able to control her anger. "Did you do something to my husband?"

"Excuse me?" He blanched, as if the idea was unimaginable.

"Ty is missing, and if I find out you're responsible I will make you pay in the worst way possible. It will make your time in the Middle East seem like a walk in the park."

His eyes lit with surprise. "I'm not sure what you're talking about."

Anger burned inside her. Cassidy didn't have time for his games.

"I'm going to check every nook and cranny of this place. I'll turn things inside out and interrogate every person until I find Ty. Am I making myself clear?"

"Unequivocally." Gilead took a step back and extended his arm in invitation. "Feel free. He's not here."

As Cassidy looked back, she noticed that everyone had returned to eating their soup. Silverware clattered on the table, but a few people still tried to steal glances at them, their curiosity getting the better of them.

"I'll be the judge of whether or not Ty is here." Cassidy took a step toward the staircase in the distance. That's where Gilead's personal living quarters and office were located. She'd start there.

"I just hate to see you wasting your time."

A moment of doubt crept into Cassidy's mind. What if Gilead was right? What if Ty was somewhere else, and he needed her?

No, that was what Gilead wanted her to think. Cassidy wouldn't be satisfied until she searched this place and saw with her own eyes that he wasn't here.

"I'm going to start in this building," Cassidy said. "You need to stay where you are, and I don't want to see you on your phone."

"Of course not."

As Cassidy took her first step up the stairs, she pulled out her phone. She hated to take this next step of action, but she had no choice. She needed more help. She needed *official* help.

Though her first inclination was to call her friend Mac, who was also a former police chief here on the island and one of Cassidy's mentors, she needed him out there running the search and rescue efforts. The person she needed helping her at Gilead's Cove had to be an officer of the law with actual jurisdiction in the area, someone who could use his connections to help her.

Without hesitating any longer, she dialed the number for Agent Gabe Abbott of the North Carolina State Bureau of Investigations. He was still in town after the last case.

Cassidy didn't fully trust the man. But she would put aside her negative feelings toward him if it meant finding Ty. She only hoped she didn't regret this.

———

CASSIDY PAUSED IN GILEAD'S OFFICE AS A CHILL SWEPT over her.

This was the man's lair. The place where his evil deeds came together. If she wasn't in such a hurry, she would carefully dissect everything here in hopes of getting into the man's psyche and figuring out what he was up to.

But she couldn't do that right now. Her only priority at the moment was finding Ty.

Gilead hadn't said anything was off-limits, so Cassidy intended to search every place possible.

After scanning his desk, she spotted a door at the back of the room.

A closet.

As she opened it, she held her breath, halfway

expecting to find Ty there. Instead, it held boxes of computer paper.

Her heart sank.

No Ty. But she still had a lot more ground to cover.

On her way out, a newspaper article that had fallen on the floor caught her eye.

She paused for just a moment. It was from a newspaper in Raleigh. In fact, it was more than an article. It was an exposé on Anthony Gilead.

Her breath caught.

Cassidy had gotten a few voice mails over the past couple of days from a reporter, but, as a rule, she stayed away from the press. In fact, Cassidy hadn't even listened to the messages until this morning, and she'd realized then that the deadline had passed.

The last thing she wanted was to have her face in the paper, especially given her history and the fact that a deadly gang had a bounty on her head. Though the initial danger was over, the reality was she'd probably never be truly safe.

Cassidy picked the paper up and scanned the text there. She read just a few lines, but they were incriminating. "Cult mastermind." "Evil in designer clothing." "A con artist preying on the weak and poor."

Gilead couldn't be happy about this. No, he wanted to present himself with a squeaky clean,

God-like image. He protected his reputation at any cost. She could only imagine the man's reaction to reading this.

But this article wasn't Cassidy's main concern at the moment.

She left his office and headed into the next door on the hallway. Gilead's apartment, it appeared. Cassidy searched under the bed, in closets, in the bathroom. No Ty.

She straightened for a minute and lifted a prayer. Her skin felt grimy with sweat and dirt. She jerked as the sound of thunder rolled in the distance again. The storm seemed to be holding offshore, threatening them with its powerful presence.

Ty, where are you? I need you, so hang on.

It was obvious he wasn't up here. But that didn't mean he wasn't at Gilead's Cove. Cassidy just needed to look harder.

She headed back down to the common area. As she did, she heard a booming charismatic voice below.

Gilead. That was Gilead.

Whom was he addressing? Was he conducting one of his sessions right now?

She paused for just a second to listen.

"You can live up to your true potential," he said. "It's a matter of mind-set. It's a decision. And you can reach this golden position in life whether you're rich or poor, beautiful or ugly. All you have to do is find that peace down deep inside you."

While Cassidy didn't disagree with his words, she questioned his motives. Everything always went back to Gilead and how he could benefit from it. He was creating a new little army of followers right now.

She paused by the stage, watching the man for a moment.

As she did, Gilead looked at her, and a grin lit his face. "Everyone, we have Police Chief Cassidy Chambers here with us today. Let's give a welcome to our guest."

In the midst of the applause, she pulled out her phone and walked to the front of the room, right below the stage. She found a picture of Ty on her cell and held it up to the faces of those in the front row.

"Has anyone seen this man?"

Everyone stared at her but said nothing.

"Look closer." Cassidy stretched out her arm, thrust her phone at everyone nearby. "Has anyone seen him?"

Again, silence was the only response.

She continued to weave among the crowd, showing his picture to everyone she could.

"Look closely, everyone," Gilead said, his voice

velvety smooth. "If you've seen him, let Police Chief Chambers know. This is someone she cares about."

A few more people acted like they were looking at the picture, but no one offered any answers or showed any recognition on their faces.

Cassidy felt a new determination rise in her. "If I find out any of you are withholding information from me, I will arrest you, and you will be charged as an accessory to the crime. Do I make myself clear?"

A slight murmur rang through the room.

Still, no one came forward.

Cassidy was wasting her time. No one was going to talk to her right now.

She had to move on.

She looked in the distance and saw Abbott step into the back of the room. He whispered something to a man at the door before looking over at her and nodding.

Good. Her backup was here.

Now she wanted to search the rest of this compound. If Ty was here, she was going to find him.

CHAPTER FOUR

AN HOUR LATER, Cassidy paused outside the Meeting Place and put her hands on her hips, trying to gather her thoughts for a moment until Abbott met her back here.

The air seemed to thicken around her as the approaching storm crept closer. She'd only noticed a few splatters of rain, but she felt sure more were on their way. The weather today was as splotchy as she'd seen it, as if Mother Nature couldn't make up her mind.

Cassidy had found no new leads.

She'd searched the Meeting Place. Every RV. Every place she could think of at the Gilead's Cove compound.

Nothing.

She'd talked to more residents as they'd dismissed from their meeting.

No one had seen Ty.

She searched the grounds for a black vehicle or trampled grass or anything else out of the ordinary.

Again, there was nothing.

Whoever had run Ty off the road was gone.

With Ty.

Cassidy pushed down the despair that wanted to rise up.

Lord, please protect him. Keep him safe. Give me clear thoughts and the wisdom to find him. Please.

Cassidy glanced over as Abbott walked toward her, coming from the water access area that bordered the compound. The man had a square face and sagging jawline, and his receding hair made his face look larger than it was. He was always brisk, with quick steps and short responses.

She tried to read his face for any sign that he'd found something when they'd split up.

His expression gave away nothing.

"Did you find anything?" Abbott paused in front her, the sleeves of his button-up shirt rolled up to his elbows and sweat dotting his forehead.

"No." She crossed her arms. "You?"

"Maybe we need to consider that Ty wasn't

abducted. Maybe Ty was never brought here to Gilead's Cove."

"I suppose that's a possibility."

Abbott leaned closer, as if to ensure no one close could overhear. "Listen, if Gilead did have something to do with this, he's too smart to have brought Ty here. You and I both know that."

Cassidy had thought about that angle, but she knew she had to rule this compound out before she could move on. It only made sense.

"I've got to find him, Abbott." The words burned her throat.

She couldn't stand around here much longer—just long enough to hear Abbott's update.

"I know," Abbott said. "What about your other guys? Did they find anything?"

Cassidy shook her head. Dane had called and given her an update a few minutes ago. "No, they searched the marsh area right around the crash site. They even got Kujo and Ranger to see if they could follow a trail. There was nothing."

Abbott's jaw tightened as he stared off in the distance. "Ty didn't just disappear. He's around somewhere. What about Gilead's other properties here on Lantern Beach?"

Cassidy frowned as she remembered the other

houses and buildings this group had purchased. She had a feeling their ultimate goal was to take over this entire island.

Nothing would stand in Anthony Gilead's way.

Not even Ty.

She held back a cry.

"We need to search those properties," Cassidy said, drawing in a shaky breath. "But I'm afraid you're right. Even if Ty was there, he's probably gone by now. I had the guys at the ferry docks searching every car before loading. The Coast Guard is also questioning any small craft leaving the island."

"We're going to find him, Cassidy."

For the first time, Abbott actually sounded halfway human.

"Thanks," she murmured, hoping he was right.

Cassidy looked up as a shadow fell over them. Anthony Gilead had stepped out of the Meeting Place and approached them. He still looked entirely too put together and arrogant for her liking.

He offered what looked like a compassionate smile. "I'm sorry that something has happened to your husband, Cassidy. If there's anything else I can do . . ."

Cassidy felt her muscles tightening, her hands fisting. What she wouldn't do to wipe that arrogant smile from the man's face . . .

"We appreciate your cooperation," Abbott said, interceding before Cassidy did something she'd regret.

A spark glimmered in Gilead's eyes. Was that satisfaction? Amusement?

Cassidy's hands fisted tighter.

"Of course," Gilead crooned. "If there's nothing else you can do here, we do have a schedule to follow."

"Where are Serena and Moriah?" Cassidy blurted.

Serena was a personal friend of Cassidy's, as well as the niece of her good friend, Skye. Moriah, on the other hand, was now Gilead's wife. Cassidy had tried over and over again to convince the woman to leave. She'd offered protection and other resources to her. But, in the end, Moriah had been blinded either by love, power, or fear.

Cassidy had searched every inch of this place, but she hadn't seen the two women. That in itself was suspicious. What if Gilead had done something to them also? She wouldn't put anything past the man.

Gilead's gaze darkened at the mention of their names, but the look faded so quickly only someone watching closely would have noticed.

"The two of them took a little trip together," he finally said.

"Where to?" Cassidy asked.

"I don't know."

"How do you not know?" Gilead was the controlling type who liked to know everything. Cassidy didn't buy his explanation. He knew something—whether the two young ladies had offered the information themselves or if he'd found it through his little spies.

"There's a process here of learning, growing, becoming disciplined, and then eventually becoming a scout—someone who reaches out and brings others into our fold. They're just doing their part in that."

Her jaw tightened. "So you have no idea where they went?"

"That's correct. I leave spiritual formation up to individuals. I only guide them."

"I don't believe you. You did something to them, didn't you? Just like you did something to Ty?"

"I don't know what you're talking about."

Cassidy couldn't keep her anger in anymore. She grabbed Gilead by his shirt and rammed him against the outer wall of the Meeting Place. He gasped and drew back as she stared at him, holding him in place.

"What do you know, Gilead?"

"Nothing."

"Yes, you do. What did you do to them? Where are they?"

"They're not here."

"Where did you put them?"

"Cassidy!" Abbott pulled her away, his eyes wide and reprimanding. "What are you doing?"

"I'm trying to find out answers."

"There are better ways."

She released Gilead and rolled her shoulders back, anger still coursing through her. The man looked entirely too smug. He knew something, didn't he? She needed to figure out a way to get that information out of him.

Gilead straightened his shirt and wiped some imaginary dirt from his sleeve. "I understand you're under some emotional distress, so I won't file charges for that assault. This time."

Her hands fisted again, but Abbott nudged her back.

Gilead stared back at her, unflinching. "I'm sorry to hear what happened. I really am."

"You have something to do with all of this," Cassidy seethed, using every ounce of self-restraint not to lunge at him again. "And I'm going to keep turning over stones until I figure out what."

Gilead's gaze held a challenge as he stared back at her. "I'm sorry to say you're going to be disappointed."

Abbott took her elbow. "Thanks again for your

cooperation. I'm sure we'll have more questions. When we do, we'll be in touch."

"Very good," Gilead said.

But the look in his eyes was pure evil—the kind that masqueraded as goodwill and kindness. That was the scariest kind of evil of all.

CHAPTER FIVE

"WHAT ARE you going to do now?" Abbott asked as they walked down the gravel lane leading away from the Meeting Place on the way back to their vehicles.

Cassidy's mind raced through all the possibilities, but it only stopped at one. "I'm going to call in everyone I know and see if they can help me find Ty. I want to scour this island until I can be certain he's not here."

"I'd do the same thing if it was someone I cared about."

She paused by Dane's police cruiser and turned toward Abbott, taking a deep breath. It was a good thing he'd been there. Otherwise, Cassidy might have done something she regretted.

"Thank you for helping, Abbott."

He offered a stiff nod. "I'm not done yet. I can head up some of the search parties. Call in some of my guys."

"I'll take all the help I can get." She studied the man's face for a moment, wondering if she truly could trust him. "You know, Abbott, maybe I was wrong about you."

"I know we got started on the wrong foot. You did the right thing by calling me." He shifted as he stood in front of her. "How about if I follow up with the properties owned by Gilead and his crew?"

That seemed like a good starting point. "That would be a huge help. I'll check on the search and rescue efforts and see if anyone's discovered anything. If you find any clues, please let me know."

"Absolutely." Abbott climbed into his sedan and pulled away from the compound, leaving a trail of dust behind his car.

For a moment, Cassidy flashed back on when Abbott had walked into the Meeting Place. He'd whispered something to the man at the door.

What was that about?

With everything that had happened, she hadn't thought to ask him. It didn't matter. She had more pressing concerns right now.

As Cassidy cranked her engine, she dialed Mac's

number, anxious to talk to her friend. She wanted his opinion. To hear his encouragement. To get his perspective.

He answered on the first ring. "Hello."

"Mac," her voice cracked.

"How are you, Cassidy?" His voice took on a fatherly tone.

"I'm hanging in."

"Any updates?"

"No, nothing. I searched all over Gilead's Cove. He's not there."

"We've been searching the area around the crash site. We haven't found any evidence leading to Ty there either."

"What about the dogs? Did they pick up on any kind of trail?" Dane had told her they hadn't earlier, but maybe there was an update.

"They did, but they lost it on the road. I'm sorry, Cassidy. I was hoping for better news."

She bit back her despair, trying desperately to stay focused. "I need you to help me get people together to search the island."

"We've already done that, Cassidy. Meet me at the police station, okay?"

"I'm on my way."

As soon as she hung up, her phone rang again.

She fully expected to hear Mac's voice on the other side as she stuck the device to her ear.

But it was a female.

"I'm trying to reach Lantern Beach Police Chief Cassidy Chambers," the voice said.

"Speaking." The caller didn't sound familiar.

"This is Arianna Stark," the woman said. "I'm a reporter with the *Raleigh Times*, and I'm doing a three-part article on Gilead's Cove. I was hoping to get a quote from you."

A quote? Cassidy didn't want her picture in the newspaper. But maybe one quote couldn't hurt. If Gilead felt the pressure coming down on him, maybe he would crack. Maybe he'd break just enough that Cassidy could find answers.

Cassidy thought about it for only a second more before nodding. "I'd love to give you a quote. What do you need to know?"

———

CASSIDY SUCKED IN A QUICK BREATH AS SHE PUT THE police cruiser in Park. There were at least a hundred people gathered in the parking lot of the police station. Many of them were her friends, but there were also a few people she didn't know—tourists, she would guess.

She glanced around for a moment and saw Wes, Braden, Austin, and Pastor Jack and his wife, Juliet. Jimmy James was there, as were real estate agent Rebecca Jarvis, EMT Tate Donovan, town musician Carter Denver, and City Manager Niles Shepherd.

Everyone had turned out to help search for Ty. It was a testament to his impact on this community.

Mac talked to them all, instructing them on how to search and what not to do. Maps of the island had been stretched out on a table so people could divide up areas. Teams were being assembled.

"Cassidy," a soft voice said behind her.

She turned and saw Lisa and Skye there. Her friends threw their arms around her.

Cassidy fought back tears as they embraced her. As tempting as it was, she couldn't crumble now. There would be time for that later.

With one more squeeze, Cassidy stepped out of their embrace. Her friends still held onto her arms, as if they didn't want to let go.

"How are you?" Lisa asked, tears welling in her eyes.

"I'm hanging in."

"We're all here for you," Skye said, her eyes also red-rimmed. "We'll do anything you need to help find Ty."

"I know you will," Cassidy said, having no doubt they would. "I really appreciate it."

"And he's strong, Cassidy," Lisa said, gripping her arm harder. "He's okay. I just know it."

"Thank you, guys," Cassidy said. "I wish I could stay and talk more, but . . ."

"We know," Skye said. "But we're here for you whenever you need us."

After muttering another thank you, Cassidy's gaze drifted over to Mac. The man was in his late sixties, with a lean, wiry build and white hair on top of his head and in his goatee. He was a character, keeping people on their toes with his antics. But when things turned serious, Mac turned all business.

The crowd around him quieted, and he waited to address them. But he looked at Cassidy first, silently asking if she wanted to join him. She had to think about it for only a moment.

"Excuse me a minute," Cassidy said.

Everyone quieted when Cassidy stepped up beside Mac. She forced a tight smile as she nodded at them. Mac went silent as he turned to her.

"Thank you everyone for coming," Cassidy said, her palms sweaty. "I can't tell you how much I appreciate this. I don't know what happened, but I do know that Ty needs your help. Desperately. Please, help me find him."

She managed to say the words without her voice cracking. But she was being torn apart inside. The more time that passed without them finding Ty, the greater the chance Cassidy wouldn't find him at all. She knew the statistics, but right now she wished she didn't. They didn't work in her favor.

Mac squeezed her arm and then took over again, relaying some final instructions. As everyone dispersed, Mac stayed behind.

"How are you holding up, kid?" he asked, his gaze oozing with concern—genuine concern.

"If I stop and let myself think about things for too long, I'll totally fall apart."

"Then let's not think too long." He directed her toward a table that had been set up just inside the station.

"No, I want to go look for him."

"I know you do. But I think you'll be better served staying here and acting as command central. All the calls will come in here. You should be here when they do—especially if someone discovers something."

His words made sense.

Cassidy paced over to the table and stared at the maps and names and phone numbers.

Mac had all of this under control.

Thank goodness.

"Tell me your version of what happened, as well as about your visit to Gilead's Cove," Mac said. "Don't leave out any details."

She recounted everything, from getting the call about the truck in the ditch to finding the blood inside Big Blue to searching Gilead's Cove for Ty. She even shared about her confrontation with Anthony Gilead and the article she'd found on his desk.

Mac leaned against the table and crossed his arms, his gaze drifting into the distance. "So let's think through the possibilities. There's a chance Ty was in a hit-and-run accident and has some type of amnesia. He could have wandered from the scene."

Cassidy frowned. "I've thought of that. But I think we would have found him by now."

"I agree." Mac nodded. "As I'm sure you've probably considered, there's a good possibility that someone grabbed him."

Hearing the words out loud caused a stab of pain in her chest, but Cassidy tried to keep her expression even. "That's right. The paint on the side of his truck and the way the trail of blood ended seems to prove that. And Gilead's Cove and the crew there are the only ones who make sense. They have the motive for grabbing him."

"Why would Anthony Gilead want Ty?"

Cassidy hadn't told Mac everything about Gilead

and Ty's past and how they might intersect. She dropped into a chair and let out a long breath. Even as she did, guilt pressed on her. She knew talking to Mac was a step in the right direction, a process that could help locate Ty. But what she really wanted was to be doing *something*. To be out in the field, looking.

Instead, she twirled her wedding ring around her finger.

"Ty thinks Gilead might have some connection with one of his past missions as a Navy SEAL," Cassidy started. "He came across a prisoner of war who had marks on his back that were very similar to the ones Gilead currently has."

"I see."

"Ty's friend Colton also remembered that there was another man on the mission. He was disguised as a terrorist, wearing the typical garb. But he had blue eyes and no weapons."

"Anthony Gilead?"

Her stomach turned just hearing his name. "That's the theory. We don't know any more than that. Of course, Gilead hasn't admitted to any of this. But the timeline makes sense. Besides, Gilead claims he was in the Middle East and found that ancient biblical book of Makir. If that's true, it puts him in the right area at the right time."

"It's all sketchy, isn't it?" Mac's jaw tightened, and he shook his head.

"Yes, it is. We're getting closer. And I have a feeling that Gilead chose this location here on Lantern Beach on purpose."

Mac did a double take at her. "Because Ty was here?"

"Exactly."

"I don't like the sound of that. Do you think Gilead is the one who sent you those texts threatening to reveal your real identity?"

Cassidy had received some threatening text messages indicating that someone knew who she really was. Detective Cady Matthews from Seattle. A woman who'd been on a hit list. How she was supposed to be dead.

The fact that someone knew that information put her at risk. If the wrong people found out Cassidy was here, her days would be limited. Everything she'd worked so hard to build would be gone.

She couldn't stomach the thought because she loved life on this little island with Ty and her friends.

"Gilead could have found out somehow," Cassidy finally said. "He's resourceful."

"He is resourceful," Mac said.

Just then, her phone rang. It was Colton. Without

thinking twice, she put the phone to her ear. "Colton, where are you?"

"I've been up on Hatteras, and I just heard about Ty. I need to talk to you, Cassidy. Now and in person."

CHAPTER SIX

COLTON TOLD Cassidy he would meet her at the police station. The minutes seemed to tick by too slowly until he arrived.

What did he know? Would the information lead her to Ty?

Cassidy prayed Colton might know something that would help in her search for her husband.

Cassidy paced the lobby area at the police station. She'd been monitoring things, acting as command central, but so far they'd heard nothing. The fact made all of this feel like a waste of time.

Finally, she spotted Colton pull up in his SUV. Mac remained by Cassidy as Colton climbed out and stepped inside the building. Her mentor seemed to sense that she needed someone close, just in case she gave into the wooziness trying to claim her.

Cassidy could see the apprehension on Colton's face as he strode toward her, and she braced herself for whatever she was about to learn. She prayed for good news.

Colton stopped in front of her. The man was tall and muscular, with blond hair styled back from his face. He had a commanding presence, and Ty had once told Cassidy that Colton was one of the best SEALs he'd ever known.

"I was talking on the phone with Ty when the line went dead," Colton started. "I had no idea this had happened. I've been trying to get up with Ty. I had a bad feeling and tried to get back as quickly as I could. It's never fast coming by ferry, though."

"What did Ty say to you?" Cassidy asked. "What did you hear?"

"I didn't hear much of anything. He mumbled, 'What's your hurry?'"

"He didn't explain what that meant?"

"I assumed that someone was riding his bumper. It sounded like an engine revved, and then everything went dead."

"He didn't say if someone was driving too close or anything?"

"No, he didn't. But that's a real possibility, now that I know he was in an accident."

Cassidy's shoulders sagged. She wasn't going to lie—she'd been hoping for something more solid.

"That's not what I wanted to tell you," Colton said, his hands going to his hips and his black T-shirt stretching across his broad chest. "Since I talked to Ty earlier about our last mission in the Middle East, I started doing some digging on the situation."

Cassidy's pulse spiked. "Okay . . ."

"He told me that this Anthony Gilead guy's real name is Gerrard Becker. I have some friends who are great investigators. Ty told me that you weren't able to leave the island because of your responsibilities here, so I figured I'd see what they could find out. I asked them to do some research for me."

"What did you find out?" Mac stepped into the conversation.

"It took a bit of work, but they managed to find an old house that Gerrard Becker's family owns out in West Virginia."

"Wait, I thought he was from Delaware?"

"He was, but he has roots back in West Virginia. Anyway, the place looked abandoned—anybody passing by would have kept on going. But my guys didn't. They went in and discovered that it looked like someone had been staying there in the not so distant past."

"And?" Cassidy could hardly wait to hear what else he'd found out.

"And this is what they found in one of the bedrooms." Colton held up his phone.

Cassidy's eyes widened when she saw the picture there. She took the phone from Colton for a better look.

Her breath caught.

Her first impression was correct. This was some kind of wall . . . full of pictures and articles about Ty.

There were photos of him and Cassidy together. Newspaper clippings mentioning the two of them. The infamous cover of *TIME* magazine that had featured Ty's silhouette as he rescued a woman from pirates off the coast of Somalia.

"This is . . . disturbing, to say the least," Cassidy mumbled. "It looks like Anthony Gilead has been researching Ty for a while now, almost to the point of obsession."

Colton raised an eyebrow, a sour expression on his face. "You can say that again. The more I learn, the more certain I am that this Gilead guy is the same person we saw dressed in terrorist garb on that mission. Maybe he was being held hostage and we didn't know it. And he developed the ultimate grudge, for lack of better terms."

"But why Ty?" Cassidy asked. "He wasn't the only one on that mission."

Colton let out a long, low breath, his eyes drifting behind Cassidy as he seemed to gather his thoughts. "I've wondered that also. Maybe Ty was the only one he recognized—and maybe it was from that article *TIME* magazine did on our team. I don't know. But it's obvious that years of bitterness and vengeance have been building."

"And now he has Ty." Cassidy's voice came out as a squeak. She drew in a deep breath and pushed away the pictures that tried to form in her mind. Horrible pictures of Ty. Being tortured. In pain. Alone.

She couldn't stomach the thought of it.

"We don't know that for sure." Mac touched her elbow, seeming to sense her distress.

"It's the only thing that makes sense." Cassidy saw no need to beat around the bush. "If Ty had a head injury and left on foot, we would have found him by now. Even if he didn't have a head injury, he was still sick from the food poisoning. He wasn't himself."

No one argued. They knew her words were true.

"You searched Gilead's Cove," Mac said. "He wasn't there."

"That's correct," Cassidy said. "Abbott is

searching the other properties Gilead's Cove owns. Gilead's too smart to have left Ty there, though."

"So what now?" Colton asked. "I'll do anything I can to help."

"I . . . I don't know. But I'm scared for Ty. I really am." She pulled her tears back. As she did, another thought slammed into her mind. "Hope House . . . Ty's next session for veterans is supposed to start tomorrow."

"Don't worry about it. I can handle things."

"Are you sure? I can start calling people to cancel."

"I've got this. You just worry about finding Ty."

Her phone rang and she saw that it was Leggott, her officer who'd quit yesterday. "Excuse me," she told Colton before putting the phone to her ear. "Leggott, what's going on?"

"Hey, Chief. I'm down here by the Preserve. There's something you need to see."

The Preserve? What exactly had he found?

The world around Cassidy seemed to come to a standstill when she heard the grimness in his voice.

"I'll be right there," she muttered.

———

CASSIDY FELT DAZED AS MAC DROVE HER POLICE SUV

down the island road. They'd passed two search and rescue teams on the way here. Both had been searching the marsh again, a somber reminder that things might not end the way Cassidy wanted them to.

She drew in a shaky breath, trying to stay focused.

Colton had stayed back at the police station to manage the command center. As a former SEAL himself, he had the tactical knowledge to make this operation work. She was grateful he was here to help her.

Kujo had stayed with him, the dog's face bearing evidence of stress and worry also. The canine could sense something was wrong.

Mac pulled into the Preserve and parked before leading her, hand on elbow, over to Leggott. The Preserve was a nature area that was bordered by the Pamlico Sound. The area was dotted with weathered live oaks with exposed roots. On each side of the beach were marsh grasses, and, bookcasing the whole scene, was a maritime forest.

She spotted Leggott in the distance, guarding the scene. Her former officer strode over to meet her.

"Chief," he said.

"Leggott," she started. "Good to see you in action again."

"I wouldn't have missed the opportunity to help you." He nodded stiffly. "Follow me."

Quietly, they walked down a sandy trail near the shoreline. A couple NCSBI agents were here—Abbott and a guy she didn't know. They'd finished searching Gilead's other island properties earlier but had found nothing.

A few people stopped and stared at Cassidy as she went past. She kept her head held high, trying her best to put on a brave front. The last thing she wanted right now was people feeling sorry for her.

Leggott stopped at the far end of the Preserve and pointed to an area of sand that had been roped off. Cassidy glanced down at the sand and paused.

This part of the beach allowed off-road driving so seeing tire tracks here wasn't abnormal. But today, the tire treads led into the water . . . and didn't come out. There was just one set going in.

"We believe these tracks match the ones on the side of the road where Ty's truck was found," Leggott said.

"So . . . you think the truck that was involved is now in the water?" Mac clarified.

"That's the theory we're working off of," Leggott said. "Abbott has called in a team that specializes in stuff like this, as well as a tow truck. We need to find out for sure."

Cassidy stood and shielded her eyes from the sun, which had begun to descend on the horizon. Behind her, dark clouds still rolled over the ocean side of the island, an occasional rumble of thunder escaping from them.

The front had caused the temperature to drop around ten degrees, and every time the wind blew, Cassidy felt it all the way down to her bones.

She stared into the blue water beyond.

She knew that someone could walk out nearly a half a mile into the Pamlico, and the water would only come waist-high. If a truck had driven into the sound, it would have to go a good distance out before it was covered.

"There's one thing about this area of the sound," Mac said, as if reading her mind.

"What's that?"

"It's mostly shallow," Mac said. "But right over there to our left, there's a deeper channel. It's where the ferry used to come in years ago. It probably goes down twelve feet right there."

Cassidy stared at the shimmering water that usually evoked peaceful feelings. Now it was like a sparkly façade concealing danger and death.

"If someone wanted to hide a vehicle, the Pamlico would be a great place to do so," Cassidy said.

"Correct."

She nodded slowly, desperate to hold herself together and act rationally. "Have we taken a cast yet of these tracks?"

"The crew from the NCSBI has been working on it," Leggott said.

She glanced around at the crowds who stared at the scene. "What about witnesses? Have you talked to anyone?"

"I did," Leggott said. "No one saw anything. This area has been surprisingly empty today. I can only assume visitors thought the storm was coming this way and stayed home."

"Right," Cassidy said.

But only one thought remained inside her head: What if Ty had been inside that truck when it went under?

She could barely stomach the thought.

CHAPTER SEVEN

THE STORM REMAINED OFFSHORE, ocean-side, teasing them with the possibility of severe weather though it remained at sea. The clouds were far enough away that the dive team felt safe proceeding with the extraction of the vehicle from the Pamlico.

Thank goodness.

Cassidy wasn't sure she would have been able to wait any longer. She would have gone into the water and searched herself if it meant finding answers.

On the west side of the island, where rescuers worked, the sun had turned glorious shades of bright pink and orange in the sky, right at the edge of the horizon. The contrast of the various sides of the island played games with her psyche. Reminded her of good and evil. Of hope and defeat. Of safety and danger.

Cassidy observed as a tow truck hauled a black truck from the water, pulling it with a winch toward the shore. She held her breath as she watched. Water drained from the vehicle's doors and bed. Seaweed clung to the sideview mirrors and tires.

And now came the moment of truth. Was this vehicle involved in Ty's crash? If so, was Ty still inside?

Mac's arm went around her shoulders, but he said nothing.

Cassidy knew there was nothing he could say. That anyone could say. If Ty was inside . . . her whole world would never be right again.

A sob nearly escaped at the thought, but she pushed it back, again chiding herself for letting her mind go there.

Drawing in a breath, along with every ounce of strength she had left in her, Cassidy took a step toward the truck. As she did, her feet seemed to take on a mind of their own, speeding up as she got closer.

Abbott stood there, near the truck, and shook his head as he peered inside.

Shook his head? What did that mean? Good news or bad?

Please let it be good news. Please.

Abbott turned to her, his expression still grim. "It's empty," he said softly. "No one is inside."

Cassidy's body nearly went limp at his announcement. Mac—who must have followed beside her—caught her elbow and held her up.

"Ty's not inside?" Cassidy clarified, her throat burning. "You're sure?"

"No, he's most definitely not." Abbott stared through the window again. "But we'll comb through everything and see what we can find. Maybe there's some evidence that will indicate what happened."

"Did you run the plates yet?" Mac asked.

"We did." Abbott looked at his phone, scrolling through something there before pausing to read. "There's a police report on it. The vehicle was stolen from up in Moyock about a week ago. The owner is an elderly man who'd stopped at a farm supply store. Left the truck running. Came back out and it was gone. The police didn't have any leads on it—until today."

"So that will lead us nowhere," Cassidy muttered.

"Not right now. But, like I said, maybe there's some evidence inside. Some fingerprints or DNA or something."

Cassidy nodded, feeling like she'd been transported into another world. A nightmarish world.

Ty. Abducted.

He was always the strong, capable one who knew how to handle himself in every situation. How could this have happened?

It was because Ty was sick, she realized. If Ty had been in his right frame of mind, no way would someone have gotten away with this.

Cassidy straightened.

"What is it?" Mac asked.

"I need to call Clemson," she muttered. Clemson was their local doctor here on the island. He also served as medical examiner as needed—which had been way too often lately.

"What are you thinking, Cassidy?" Mac asked, studying her face.

"I'll tell you in one minute." She dialed Clemson's number, and he answered on the first ring.

"Cassidy . . . I've been over here praying. I wish I could leave and help but, unfortunately, I have patients. Any news?"

"No sign of Ty yet," she told him. "But I have a question. How long did most people's bout of food poisoning last?"

"Hmm . . . It seemed to peak at about eight hours after eating that salad dressing at the party. Why?"

Eight hours? She let that sink in a moment. "I told you Ty wasn't feeling well."

"Yes, I told him he should come in to the clinic to be checked out, but he said he was fine."

"Clemson, he didn't seem to be getting better. In fact, he almost seemed worse."

The doctor paused then said, "Are you saying what I think you're saying?"

"I'm just wondering if Ty had a different kind of poisoning from everyone else. Not salmonella, but something else, something more . . . potent. Deadly."

"It's a possibility, Cassidy. Without seeing him, I can't rule it out."

The bad feeling in Cassidy's gut grew worse by the moment. "Thanks, Clemson."

"I'm praying for you, Cassidy. And for Ty also."

"Don't stop."

Cassidy's thoughts raced as she walked away. She needed to talk to Melva and find out exactly what the woman had put in Ty's coffee. She was the only one who knew the answer.

But would she talk?

Cassidy was going to have to go through the FBI to find out.

———

TY JERKED HIS EYES OPEN, EXPECTING LIGHT AND clarity and a sense of place.

Maybe a hospital bed. That would explain the pain pulsating through his body. The ache that consumed his muscles. The clamminess of his skin and the grogginess of his thoughts.

Instead, darkness stared back—an all-encompassing black that couldn't be penetrated or interpreted. It was like an inky abyss surrounded him.

A soft moan escaped from his parted lips as he realized he wasn't lying down at all. No, he was standing, though barely.

He stretched his hand forward to feel what was around him.

Only he couldn't.

His left arm was attached to . . . what was that?

He tugged his arm again.

A cuff of some sort clamped around his wrist, hanging near his head. With his other hand, he reached over and felt the thick metal circle there. It appeared to be welded to a thick chain.

Ty reached as high as he could, trying to feel where the chain led.

After following about a foot of links, the chain ended at the wall above his head.

This was like a jail cell, he realized. Only this place was no official prison. Instead, it seemed more like a medieval torture chamber.

His arm tingled, all the blood obviously long gone.

He must have passed out in this position.

But for how long? How long had he been here?

He reminded himself to stay focused and concentrate on solutions. SEAL training had taught him that. He couldn't give in to the pain that wanted to consume him—unless he wanted to die here.

And he most definitely did not want to die.

Quickly, Ty took an inventory of himself and his surroundings.

He was consumed by blackness. His arm was chained to a wall. His head pounded furiously, the ache there beyond normal.

He sucked in a breath as memories began to flash through his mind.

That truck had run him off the road. Everything had gone black.

And now Ty was here.

But where was here?

The space around him smelled dank, like Ty was underground. And the wall was rough, like it was partially made from mortar and partly from cinder blocks. It was almost like a basement . . . only the island's water level was so high that none of the homes here had basements.

He tugged at the chain again, hoping it might give.

No luck. It was attached firmly to the wall. No way would he be pulling it free without breaking some bones.

Another thought slammed into his head.

Cassidy.

Where was Cassidy right now? Had someone grabbed her also?

Ty's stomach twisted at the thought. It was one thing for him to suffer, and an entirely different situation if it was the woman he loved who needed help.

Please help her to be okay, Lord.

But he knew that even if Cassidy was physically okay, she'd be an emotional wreck when she realized he was missing. Ty had no idea how long he'd been here, but certainly it was long enough that Cassidy had realized he was gone. Someone had to have reported his truck by now.

A sound in the distance made him freeze.

Someone—or something—else was in here.

Did Ty even want to know?

A new round of nausea rose in him. His sickness . . . it still plagued his system. His skin felt clammy, and his muscles ached.

Ty was going to have trouble defending himself

right now. He was going to have to draw on every ounce of his military training to get out of this situation alive.

And he would do exactly that . . . for Cassidy's sake.

CHAPTER EIGHT

"MAYBE YOU SHOULD GO HOME, CASSIDY." Mac squeezed her arm as they remained at the Preserve, watching as the NCSBI loaded the water-drenched vehicle onto a flatbed tow truck. "Try to get some rest."

"There's no way I can rest knowing that Ty is out there somewhere."

It had been only eight hours since the accident happened. With every second that passed, Ty could be getting farther and farther away. It wasn't okay. Every minute counted right now.

"I figured you'd say that. But you're not going to be worth anything if you don't get some sleep." Mac gave her a pointed look. "Believe me. I know. Besides, I don't know what else we can do tonight.

Until we have more daylight, it's going to be hard to search."

"I think every inch of the island has already been scoured." Defeat lined Cassidy's voice, and she leaned against her SUV, exhaustion pressing on her.

Mac slipped his arm around her shoulders. "Don't give up hope, Cassidy."

"I'm not sure if I'm out of hope or out of ideas. I don't know where else to look, Mac. I don't know how to find Ty." She squeezed her eyes shut and pinched the skin above her nose. "If he were in my shoes, he would know exactly what to do. I can't let him down."

"I don't think you could let him down if you tried. He looks at you like you stepped right out of his dreams and into his life. I don't think I've ever seen someone look so smitten."

A small smile tried to tug at her lips. "I know that he loves me."

"He does." Mac straightened, seeming to snap out of his somber thoughts. "How about this? I'll go grab some food. You do need to eat. Then I'll meet you back at the police station, and we can try to look at this investigation from a different angle—from every angle we can think of. How does that sound?"

Cassidy nodded, relieved that she'd have Mac there helping her, taking on the urgency of the situation with her. "It sounds great, Mac. Colton is still there working on a few things also. Maybe he can help."

"I certainly won't turn down help from a former SEAL. Do you want me to drop you off first?"

She shrugged. "Actually, I could use a moment alone."

"You'll be okay driving?"

"I think so."

"Okay, I'll catch a ride with Leggott then. He's ready to leave too. I'll see you there in about twenty minutes."

Cassidy climbed into her SUV and sat back, drawing in deep breaths and releasing them over and over again.

In the distance, she saw Abbott directing his men on how to handle the truck. She'd already glanced inside, but she couldn't tell anything. No, they would take it back to the lot located behind the police station. It was fenced, and they could examine the vehicle all they needed there.

Most of the gawkers had left as darkness fell. The last update she'd heard hadn't offered any new information. It seemed like they were ruling out the entire island . . . which didn't make Cassidy feel any better.

It was her first moment alone since she'd gone to Gilead's Cove.

As she glanced down at the wedding ring on her finger, the first tears escaped from her eyes and rolled down her cheeks.

Ty.

He'd made everything that was wrong with her world right. Her first impression of the man had been so entirely incorrect. She'd thought he was arrogant and crass when really he was anything but. Cassidy discovered a man much different than the rich crowd she'd been raised around, who'd grown up with silver spoons in their mouths.

Ty put others before himself. He looked out for the ones he loved. He enjoyed the simple things in life. He cared more about people than things.

Marrying him had been the best decision she'd ever made.

She twisted the ring on her finger, remembering the day she and Ty got married on the beach. It had been the best day of her life. All her friends had been there. Mac had given her away. Pastor Jack had married them.

Even the sun had cooperated, spreading beautiful colors across the evening sky.

Cassidy drew in a deep breath, trying to think like Ty. He would tell her to focus on the solution, not the problem. That's what she needed to do right now.

But every conclusion and solution led back to Anthony Gilead.

Cassidy firmly believed the man was capable of killing Ty. She knew the possibility that she'd never see her husband again was very real.

The realization broke her heart into a million pieces.

She buried her face in her hands as the tears came harder.

She needed to release her sobs for a moment. And, when she was done, she needed to be ready to lead her team on what might be her most important investigation of all: finding her husband.

———

CASSIDY WALKED INTO THE STATION AND SAW A GROUP still remained. Colton, Dane, Leggott, and Braden bent over a table in Dane's office, looking at what appeared to be a map of the island.

When they spotted her, they looked up, compassion in their gaze as they straightened with respect.

She paused in the doorway and gathered her thoughts. "You're all still working?"

"We wouldn't leave you at a time like this, Chief," Dane said.

She wiped beneath her eyes, wondering if they

were red. Wondering if her guys knew she'd been crying. It didn't matter now. She had more important things to worry about.

"Leggott, you back on the force?" She turned to her officer who had just quit.

"I'm not going to leave when you need me. I'll stick around until Ty is found." He nodded like a soldier talking to a commanding officer.

"I appreciate it." She turned to Braden. "And you're starting early?"

"Only if it's okay with you. I figured you could use an extra hand around here."

"Of course, it's okay with me." Her gaze stopped at Colton. "Any updates I should know about?"

With a grim frown, he shook his head. "Nothing. All the search parties came back with no new leads. We've talked to people in town. No one has seen anything. And, so far, the truck hasn't turned up anything either. Abbott came in a couple times from the back lot where he and his team are analyzing both Ty's truck and the one pulled from the Pamlico. He said he'll keep us apprised."

Cassidy drew in a deep breath. It wasn't the news she wanted to hear, but, at the same time, it didn't surprise her. That simply meant she needed to recalculate.

She nodded at the desk. "What are you guys looking at?"

"We're trying to figure out if there's any area of the island we haven't searched yet," Dane said. "We're marking off the areas we know for sure have been investigated."

"Did you find anything?" She peered at the map, hoping for something that jumped out.

Dane pointed to an area near the bottom of the map. They'd marked an X there.

"This is where we found Ty's truck. And this is the Preserve, where we found the truck that we believe ran him off the road." He pointed to a different area about a mile north on the island. "There wasn't much time between when his truck was discovered and when we got on the scene. It's my personal belief that whoever may have grabbed him couldn't have gotten far."

"But whoever did this got that truck in the water at the Preserve without anyone noticing," Cassidy said, trying to think the scene through. "This person had to have done that after I called the Coast Guard. What if the person behind this put Ty on a boat and got him off this island?"

The words caused a new cascade of emotions inside her. If they did that, Ty could be anywhere by now. She might not ever find him.

"I guess we shouldn't rule anything out," Braden said. "But I think the Coast Guard would have seen Ty if he'd been on a boat. I saw several of their boats out there patrolling the island. I doubt anyone slipped past."

"I suppose someone could have taken him to one of the houses on the island," Leggott said. "Only about half of them are occupied right now. We've been in touch with the rental companies, and they're cooperating with us."

"Good." The rental companies . . . it was thanks to them that Cassidy had been found when she'd been abducted by a gunman not long ago.

She now understood what Ty had gone through when he'd searched for her.

"We plan on continuing to look at the empty rental houses through the night," Leggott continued.

"It's somewhere to start." A little hope returned to Cassidy. Maybe every road wasn't a dead end. And she was entirely grateful for such a great support system.

Braden shifted, studying her face. "You think Anthony Gilead is behind this, don't you?"

She hesitated only a second before nodding. There was no need to try to be politically correct. She needed to speak from her heart. "Yes, I do. But I don't have enough evidence to arrest him yet. I need to find something that ties Gilead with Ty's disappearance."

"We'll find you some, Chief," Dane said. "We'll find you some."

Just as he said the words, the door opened and Mac stepped in, two bags of food in his hands. Now the whole crew was here.

Cassidy felt a second wind coming on.

"Let's get to work, everyone!" Mac said, dropping the bags on the desk. "We don't have any time to waste."

CHAPTER NINE

MORIAH HEARD movement across the vast abyss where she was held captive.

Was Ty waking up? Was he okay?

She'd seen two men bring him down here about an hour ago. Not bringing. They'd *dragged* him.

Ty hadn't been conscious. He'd looked half dead, for that matter.

Blood had streamed from his forehead. His skin had looked pale. He'd moaned as if in intense pain.

Serena had let out a terrible cry beside her when she saw her friend in that state.

Witnessing all of this only solidified Moriah's realization: whatever was happening here at Gilead's Cove, it was bad. Much worse than she'd ever imagined. People's lives were on the line.

"Ty, are you awake?" Serena asked, her voice rushed and urgent.

He let out a sound that seemed nearly inhuman before finally asking in a throaty voice, "Serena?"

"Yes! It's me! I'm so glad you're okay, Ty. I was so worried."

"I feel like I've been run over." His hoarse voice was tinged with agony. "Where are we? Do you know?"

"We're in an old bunker not far from Gilead's Cove," Serena said.

"An old bunker? I should have known," Ty said. "Is it just you down here?"

Moriah cleared her throat, desperate not to be forgotten. "I'm here too. It's Moriah."

She heard his chain clank. He must be pulling it, trying to get it down. Soon, he would learn it was no use. Not even Superman could break through those heavy chains.

He let out another groan, one that reeked of pain and suffering.

Moriah's heart skipped a beat, the sound making her chest tighten with even more anxiety. "Are you all right?"

"I don't . . . I don't feel well. I have a fever. Food poisoning. I must have hit my head when that man ran me off the road."

Her heart thudded in her ears as his words sank in.

Had Gilead brought him down here to die? Had he left *all* of them here to die? Because there was no way Moriah could return to regular life at the compound after this. She knew too much now. Gilead would never let her have any freedom.

She'd been a fool to ever think he would. She'd been a fool to fall for any of this, for that matter.

When she'd first driven off the ferry and onto Lantern Beach, she'd been full of so much hope that she'd get a fresh start and change her life. Well, she sure had changed her life. From the moment Anthony Gilead had set his sights on her, nothing had been okay. Moriah had just been too stupid to see it.

Instead, she'd justified his actions. Pretended things would change. And that had been her biggest mistake of all.

"We need to figure out a way out of here," Serena said.

"What are you thinking?" Ty asked, his voice sounding weaker by the moment.

"I don't know," Serena said. "Maybe we could make a lot of noise. Maybe someone would hear us."

"You know as well as I do that we're in the middle of nowhere," Moriah said. "No one will hear us. Besides, the walls are thick and covered by sand and dirt. We'd be wasting our breath."

"What are these walls made out of?" Ty asked.

"I think they're cinder blocks," Moriah said, remembering how they'd looked and felt. "The chains have been cemented or welded in."

"Is there anything else in here?" Ty asked. "Anything to stand on? To use as a weapon?"

Moriah glanced around, desperately wishing some light would cut through the darkness. But it didn't. All she saw was a void that reminded her of her future—pointless.

"I haven't been able to find anything," Moriah said. "Although, when the door was open earlier, I think I might have seen an old crate against the wall. I doubt I can reach it."

"Can you try?" Ty asked. "At least it would be something."

"Maybe." A jolt of fear rushed through her. Moriah didn't know why she felt so scared or nervous. There was just something about the darkness. About reaching into the unknown. It creeped her out. Everything felt scary right now.

With one wrist still attached to the wall, Moriah slid her leg forward and waved it in the air, hoping she would touch something. This room wasn't incredibly big. If she had to guess, it was maybe twelve feet across. But still, with her limited mobility, reaching anything was going to be hard.

"Any luck?" Ty asked.

"Not yet." Her voice escaped with a hitch as she stretched herself farther. Finally, her foot hit something—but just barely. It could have been a crate. Maybe.

"I heard something," Serena said, her pitch rising with excitement. "Did you touch something?"

"I think I might have. Let me stretch a little farther." She extended her leg, trying to locate the object again. But it was so far away. She let out a gasp as pain shot through her wrist. Her skin felt raw and blistered, and the cuff tugging against it only exacerbated her pain.

"Are you okay, Moriah?" Ty asked. "Did something happen?"

"I'll be fine." She must be bruised. Something might even break. But it was better than being dead.

Her foot hit the mystery object again. But instead of pulling it toward her, she accidentally shoved it farther away.

No!

She reached as far as she could, desperate to do something that would fuel their chances of escape. As her skin pulled against the metal, another moan escaped.

"It's okay, Moriah," Ty said. "You don't have to hurt yourself."

His voice sounded so soothing. It was how Moriah had imagined her husband might sound. That he'd be a gentle leader. A patient one. Someone who cared.

Her first—and second—husbands had been anything but. At twenty-three, she felt shame to admit she'd made not one but two poor choices when choosing her life mate. Then again, she'd always had bad taste in men, from the time she'd first become interested in the opposite sex in eighth grade.

Dirk Jacobson had been her first kiss. He'd set it up so all the boys were watching around the corner when he copped a feel.

A surge of jealousy swept through her as she remembered Ty's calm demeanor. She wanted someone like him in her life. She wanted someone who would love and treasure her for who she was.

But Moriah wasn't sure that would ever be in her future. She'd made too many mistakes. There was too much she'd done wrong. She wasn't sure it was possible to recover.

"I'm sorry," she muttered, giving it one last try. "But I can't reach it. It may be closer to you now, though."

"I'll see if I can get it," Ty said. "Maybe we can use it to get out of here. Somehow."

"But how?" How would an old wooden crate help secure their escape?

"Maybe there's a nail in it. Maybe I can stand on it and work this cuff a little more. I don't know."

Moriah's mind raced as she tried to remember everything she could about Ty. "You were a SEAL, right?"

"That's right," Ty said. "Did your husband talk about me?"

Moriah briefly considered her response. She felt no loyalty to Gilead anymore, no guilt in sharing things she'd seen or heard. Maybe Ty needed to know what she did. "No, he didn't really talk about you. But I saw information about your wife on Gilead's computer."

Ty said nothing for a minute. "Is that right? Exactly what was on his computer about Cassidy?"

Her statement must have been shocking. There was so much Moriah could share. But she had to pick only the most important information right now.

"Just some old articles," Moriah said. "I never really understood why Gilead had them up on his screen, almost like he was researching her. Honestly, I just assumed he liked her. *Liked* her liked her. I . . . well, I felt jealous. It's one of the reasons I didn't like your wife. It was shallow. I just didn't see it at the time."

"Your husband is a dangerous man, Moriah."

"I'm learning that." Silence fell for a minute, and Moriah wondered what else she should say. "I also saw that he got a life insurance check for my ex-husband."

"What?" Ty asked, his voice filled with surprise.

"It's true. Somehow, Gilead got it sent here without my knowledge."

"And he didn't even tell you?"

"No, he didn't. Looking back now, I can only assume he kept the money himself to help pay his bills at this place." A cry escaped from the depths of her. Moriah had been so stupid to think things would change when she got here. So, so stupid.

"He's really good at letting people see what he wants them to see," Ty said, his voice taking on a soothing tone again.

"Why does he hate you so much?" Moriah was trying to put the pieces together. "What happened between you?"

"I'm not sure, but I think we're somehow connected from our time in the Middle East."

The Middle East . . . Ty being a SEAL . . . did Gilead coming here to Lantern Beach have more to do with Gilead's personal life than he ever let on?

He'd said he chose this location because God had led him here. The rugged landscape would bring people back to their roots, he'd said. It would help them connect with their maker and feel God's vastness as they looked out over the water.

It was a lie. Every word out of Anthony Gilead's mouth was a lie.

"Is that how he got those awful scars on his back?" Moriah finally asked.

"I think so."

"Why would he even have been over in the Middle East?"

"Probably because he was looking for the ancient scrolls of Makir. At least, maybe that was part of it. You know his real name is Gerrard Becker. He's like a totally different person now. He reinvented himself."

"Gerrard Becker?" The name didn't even sound right as it rolled off Moriah's tongue. He had really been a totally different person with a totally different life? He'd given no hints of it. She'd just assumed he'd always been the charismatic man people worshipped.

"That's right," Ty said. "Anthony Gilead is originally from Delaware. He's been married at least two other times. He pastored a small church."

"No . . ." Had her husband once lived a normal life? Had he been a shirt and tie, hell-fire-and-brimstone preacher? Moriah imagined a small country church with enthusiastic congregants hanging on his every word.

"It's true."

"Why would he change his mind and become this . . . this . . . cult leader?" It was the first time Moriah had said the word out loud. *Cult*. But that's what all of this was. Anthony Gilead was a cult leader.

"That's what we're trying to figure out also. We have no idea what caused the switch. I was hoping you might know."

"I wish I could tell you something. But this is all news to me."

Just then, the door opened above them. Moriah squinted against the bright light.

A tall, broad figure came down the steps.

It was Enoch, another of Gilead's right-hand men. He didn't look at anyone else. Just Moriah.

He said nothing. Only unlocked her cuff and took her wrist. He squeezed her injured wrist, despite the fact that she gasped with pain.

"You need to come with me," he said, pulling her toward the steps.

Another surge of fear captured her. Suddenly, staying down here in the dark, dank place seemed like a better alternative to whatever waited above.

"Let her go!" Ty yelled.

His chain clanked against the wall as he tried to break loose.

But Moriah had no choice. Enoch's grip was iron-clad. She couldn't get away.

She looked back at Ty and Serena one more time before she reached the world above, and she braced herself to face whatever waited ahead.

CHAPTER TEN

CASSIDY DOWNED another cup of coffee, her head pounding from lack of sleep and the rise and fall of her adrenaline surges.

She'd stayed up all night, reviewing everything she could and trying to find answers. Mac, Colton, Wes, and Austin had stayed with her for most of the night. They'd talked tactical operations in another room. On occasion, Cassidy had stuck her head in the room and joined them.

She wasn't as much of a tactical girl as she was one who got lost in her thoughts as she solved crimes.

Her quest had almost turned neurotic as she looked at the same information over and over again. For a few hours in the middle of the night, she'd even driven around the island. She'd gone back to the scene of the accident. Had driven past Gilead's Cove. She'd even stopped by the Preserve and looked at the area where the truck had gone into the water.

All while searching for a clue. For something she hadn't noticed before. For any sign of Ty.

There had been nothing.

Cassidy rubbed the skin between her eyes as she leaned into her desk.

Where could Ty be?

That's what she would figure out today.

With that thought, she pulled her eyes open. The window behind her displayed the rising sun. Just like yesterday, sketchy weather was in the forecast with periods of scattered showers and thunderstorms, dotted with moments of sunshine and blue skies.

They had to find Ty today. They had to.

A couple leads had been called in last night, but they'd turned up nothing. A light on in an unrented house turned out to be on a timer. A weird sound behind someone else's house turned out to be a stray dog.

Nothing.

Phone calls were coming in already this morning. Dane had come in to answer them for her.

She picked up the newspaper in front of her again

and read more of the article that Arianna Stark had written. The piece left no room for doubt that Anthony Gilead was an evil, twisted man.

But reading the article gave Cassidy pause. What if Arianna used her quote? What if, instead of driving Gilead out of hiding, it caused him to take revenge on Ty?

Cassidy prayed her plan didn't backfire. The newest edition of the newspaper hadn't been released yet, but she wondered what today's article would hold.

As she heard the door open again, she rose, checking to see who had come in.

It was Wes O'Neill. He was a part-time plumber, part-time kayaking guide here on the island . . . and a certified bachelor. Of all the people here, Wes was probably Ty's best friend. He looked nearly as worried as Cassidy felt.

He frowned when he spotted Cassidy across the room. With quick steps, he met her and gave a friendly hug. Stepping back, he held up a brown paper bag and a cup of coffee.

"These are from Lisa," he said.

Cassidy took them from him. "Thank you."

"How are you holding up?" he asked, his eyes full of concern.

They stood in the lobby, but Cassidy nearly felt like she was living an out of body experience. Sometimes, this all felt like a bad dream. Other times, reality hit her hard, nearly knocking her off her feet.

"About as well as can be expected, I suppose." There was no need to skirt around the truth. Wes knew that as well as she did.

"I'm sorry, Cassidy. Anything you need us to do, we're there for you. You know that, right?"

She squeezed his arm. "I do, Wes. Thank you. I won't hesitate to call."

He squinted as he stared at her, obviously not ready to leave yet. "Did you get any sleep last night?"

"No, I didn't. I had too much to do."

"Do you need to rest some?"

Cassidy waved him off. "I'll be fine. But thank you for your concern."

They both pivoted as the front door opened again and a pretty redhead stepped inside. The woman smiled nervously when she saw Cassidy and Wes staring and waved her hand in the air.

"I have a feeling this is a bad time," she started with a nervous frown.

"Can I help you?" Cassidy asked, noticing the paper in her hands.

"I came to apply for the job of dispatcher," she started, holding up the paper. "I heard there was an opening. I just happen to be new in town, and I need a job. I know I already dropped off an application yesterday, but I thought I'd bring another one, just in case the first one got lost."

She handed Cassidy her resumé, and Cassidy scanned it quickly. The woman was twenty-five years old and had held down two jobs since she graduated from college. She had glowing letters of recommendation and boasted a 3.8 GPA.

"Why did you come to Lantern Beach?" Cassidy glanced up, trying to get a feel for the woman.

"Change of pace." The woman extended her hand. "I'm Paige, by the way. Paige Henderson."

"I'm Chief Chambers," Cassidy said before pointing with her thumb to the man beside her. "This is my friend, Wes."

Wes smiled, his gaze fastened on the woman. "Nice to meet you."

Cassidy did a double take. Wait . . . Wes was staring at the woman. He thought she was pretty, didn't he? It was the first time Cassidy had seen Wes appear to be even mildly interested in anyone. He was usually more standoffish with women.

"Nice to meet you both," Paige said, rubbing her

hands on her jeans. "Is this a bad time? I can come again later."

"No, wait." Cassidy continued reading her resumé. "You used to work for Fish and Wildlife down in Florida?"

"That's right. I did dispatch for them. I loved living down there, and it was a great job. Unfortunately, I followed a boyfriend up to Wilmington, and he dumped me. I decided to stay in North Carolina and make the best of it, though."

"I'll need to a do a background check," Cassidy started. "But we're in desperate need of someone to help us out here. If you're free, you can consider yourself provisionally hired."

Her eyes lit with surprise. "Really? Oh, that would be wonderful. Otherwise, I'd have to apply for jobs as a waitress, and I'm so clumsy that I'd be terrible at it."

"Can you start now?" Cassidy hoped this woman wasn't connected with Gilead's Cove. She would get Dane to do some digging, just in case. She couldn't take any chances.

Paige put her purse on the counter. "Yes, I can. I'd love to."

Cassidy took a step back. "Listen, I have some other things I need to do right now. But you'll need to get acquainted with who's who in the town. Wes, would you mind giving her a rundown? Making her feel welcome?"

He raised his eyebrows before shrugging in a laid-back manner. "Yeah, sure. I'd be happy to. Whatever helps you out."

"Great. I'll be in my office for a little while. I need to make some calls, so I prefer not to be disturbed unless absolutely necessary."

"Of course," Paige said. "I'm a fast learner."

"Welcome aboard."

———

BACK IN HER OFFICE, CASSIDY PICKED UP THE PHONE and made a split-second decision to call Kaleb Walker. He was a member of Gilead's Cove and a lawyer. But Cassidy had helped him out by locating his sister not long ago—his sister who just happened to be Gilead's second wife. The investigation had built some rapport between Cassidy and Kaleb, and she hoped that worked to her advantage now.

However, Cassidy knew it was risky to call him.

After four rings, he answered in a raspy, rushed whisper, "Hello?"

"Kaleb, it's Cassidy Chambers."

"Yeah, I know, I recognized the number. I told you not to call me. Am I going to have to change my number?" He didn't sound happy, but Cassidy didn't care.

"I need your help."

He went silent a minute as if his thoughts had to catch up with the conversation. "I heard you were out here earlier."

"Where were you?"

"I went to Ocracoke this morning to meet with a couple people interested in the Cause."

"My husband is missing. I think Gilead has something to do with it. I need your help."

"I don't know what I can do."

"Have you seen Ty?" No way was Cassidy letting this conversation end that easily.

"No, I haven't seen him here. I don't know why you want to blame everything on Gilead. It's like you have a vendetta toward us."

"I just want to find my husband." Her voice quivered. "Just like you wanted to find your sister."

He let out a long sigh. "Yeah, I get that. But I'm not sure what you expect me to do. I haven't seen him."

"Can you poke around? See if you can find anything out? Please. Maybe someone there has seen him."

Again, he went silent before finally blurting, "I'm sticking my neck out for you, you know."

"I know." Cassidy prayed he would say yes.

"But I'll see what I can find out. Expect it to be nothing. Your husband probably isn't here. Maybe he just ran off. Or maybe he was involved with a crime that has nothing to do with Gilead's Cove. You'd be wise to broaden your search."

"You're right. That could be the case. But I need to know for sure that I can rule out Anthony Gilead, and you're the only one who can help me."

He let out another long sigh. "Give me a few hours. I'll be in touch. Don't call me. I'll call you."

Before Cassidy could say anything else, the line went dead. Kaleb had ended the call. She lowered the phone back to the desk and sighed. At least it was something.

She glanced at her watch. In an hour, everyone would be gathering again. They would divide up and search the island again. Mac was coordinating the efforts himself, and Colton was helping him.

Colton had also called in a few of his former military buddies who'd been on his SEAL team. If anyone could help find Ty, they could. They'd trained their whole lives for things like this.

Please, Lord. Help me to find him. Please. Help him to be okay.

Just as Cassidy muttered "amen," a soft knock sounded at her door. A wide-eyed Paige Henderson stood there, looking apprehensive about disturbing Cassidy so soon on her first day on the job.

"Chief, I know you said not to bother you," she started. "But someone's here to see you, and I don't think you're going to want to pass this up. At least, that's what Wes said."

CHAPTER ELEVEN

TY TRIED to ignore the ache in his body. Ignore the sickness that wanted to claim him.

But he was struggling to focus. His heart hammered. His fever had spiked again.

He had to draw on every ounce of his strength right now if he wanted to get out of here alive. He'd have time to recover from this food poisoning later. He prayed that was the case, at least.

In the distance, he could hear Serena softly crying. He didn't know how much time had passed since Moriah had been taken away. If he had to guess, it was an hour or so. Serena had taken it hard.

Surges of anger still went through Ty at the memory of how everything had played out. They'd been left in the dank, old bunker. Without food. Without water.

His friends Jack and Juliet had also been locked into one of these not long ago. There must be more than one on the island. Would anyone even think to look for something like this?

His guess was no.

"Serena, what happened?" Ty asked. "Why did you come here to Gilead's Cove?"

"I wanted to find information for you," Serena said. "I wanted to help, to be useful."

Ty squeezed his eyes shut. "We begged you not to do that."

"I know. But . . ." Her voice trailed. "I just felt like I was best positioned to do it. Especially with Dietrich . . ."

"Sweetheart, I hate to break this to you, but Dietrich would probably kill you if he had the chance."

Serena remained quiet a minute. Ty wished he could see her face, her reaction. But the utter darkness had returned.

"You don't know that," Serena finally said, her voice weaker than ever. "Dietrich acts like he's sold out to the Cause, but he's not."

"How do you know that?"

"Because I can see it in his eyes."

Ty didn't want to refute Serena's statement. He heard the hope in her voice. But the girl was naïve and sometimes only saw what she wanted to see. Dietrich was in this just as deep as everyone else.

"How are we going to get out of here, Ty?" Serena's voice held a tremble.

Good. While he didn't want her to be frightened, this situation *was* frightening. She needed to realize how serious this was. Fear could keep her alive.

But he had to be honest. "I don't know, Serena."

Silence stretched for a moment. Occasionally, Ty thought he heard something outside. The wind maybe? Just a little earlier he'd wondered if he heard thunder.

"I hate the dark," Serena said. "I hate being down here. I've never been so terrified, Ty."

The girl had definitely gotten herself in over her head.

"Just pretend like the darkness is your friend. Pretend like it's something you can conquer."

"What do you mean?" Serena asked.

He thought back to his training. It was just as much about mental toughness as it was being physically capable and strong. "That's what I always did when I was a SEAL. Whenever something seemed frightening, I just tried to reframe it as a challenge."

"Wait, even Navy SEALs get frightened?"

He wanted to smile but couldn't. "Yes, even SEALs get frightened sometimes. It's human nature when you're in a situation where your life is on the line. Fight or flight."

"And you always chose to fight."

"It was my job to choose to fight—most of the time, at least."

"You were probably born a fighter."

Ty said nothing. Serena was probably right. Some people were natural born warriors. He'd always had an instinct for standing up for others. For standing up for justice.

And Ty wouldn't go down without a fight. Not right now. Even with the sickness ravaging his body. With his arm numb. With an ache pounding his head.

No, he needed to go home to Cassidy.

He had new guests coming in to take part in Hope House retreat center. Was that today? Ty had lost track of day and night down here in this dungeon.

He had plans for his future—plans that God could give or take way. But Ty was going to operate on the faith that he still had a future left here on this earth. And that if he didn't . . .

Well, he couldn't stomach that thought right now. Ty knew only that he tried to live with no regrets, knowing his days—like everyone's—were numbered.

But he'd be lying if he didn't admit to himself that he wanted a future with Cassidy that included children and growing old together. He wanted that more than anything.

"I don't want to die like this, Ty." Serena's voice cracked again.

Ty could hear her tears—hear the sniffles, the anguish in her words. Moriah being taken away had shaken her up.

"Don't give up hope, Serena," he told her. "It's not over until it's over."

"I think . . . I think my wrist is broken. It's hurts so much."

"We'll get you help soon. When we get out of here."

She sniffled again, but it sounded like she was trying to control her sobs. After a couple of minutes, she said, "I used to have a crush on you, you know."

Ty raised his eyebrows at the change of subject. He wasn't even sure how to respond to that. "Did you?"

"Of course, every girl on this island probably did. You were the dashing Navy SEAL with a kind heart and a cute dog and an awesome truck. What's there not to love about that?"

"I . . . don't know what to say." Ty reached up and tugged at the cuff around his wrist, trying to ease some of the soreness there. The device had cut into part of his skin and rubbed the rest of it raw.

"And see that? You're humble too."

He gave the chain another tug, but it was no use. Ty already knew that. But he couldn't stand not doing anything.

He turned his attention back to Serena. "Serena, life has a lot to offer you. You're always full of surprises, you're enthusiastic, you work hard. We're going to get through this. You're going to get out of here, meet a nice guy—who isn't Dietrich—and figure out the rest of your life."

She sniffled again. "I wish I felt that sure."

As she said the words, the doors above them opened.

Ty's breath hitched. Who was here this time? And what were they planning?

Adrenaline surged through Ty's muscles as he tried to prepare himself for what was to come.

Speaking of the devil . . . Dietrich slowly came into view as he sauntered down the stairs.

The man didn't even look at Ty. Instead, he walked right to Serena, holding something in his hand.

A key.

He unlocked the cuff around her wrist but didn't appear to be rescuing her. No, Dietrich wasn't moving fast enough or with any urgency.

"What are you doing, Dietrich?" Serena asked, her voice weak and desperate.

"I'm following orders."

"Orders to do what?" Ty's voice cut through the room. He wanted to protect her, but he couldn't. Not with this cuff around his wrist.

"Orders to retrieve Serena and to not ask any more questions." Dietrich's voice remained dull.

Had he been drugged? The man just seemed out of it.

"What about Ty? You can't just leave him here." Serena rubbed her wrist, her eyes wide as she looked back at Ty. Dietrich's hand circled her bicep, but Serena pulled away, trying to get out of his grasp and reach Ty.

It was no use. Dietrich picked her up and threw her over his shoulder.

"Like I said, I don't ask questions. I just do as I'm told."

Serena glanced over at Ty as Dietrich hauled her up the stairs. Tears streamed down her face as she mouthed, "I'm sorry."

Ty tugged against his chain again, desperation surging in him. He had to help Serena.

But the chain didn't give. He wasn't going anywhere.

He'd been captured by the enemy. He was a prisoner of war—only this war was different than any he'd ever fought before. It was on American soil.

Yet it was the same. This leader might as well be a terrorist. He'd brainwashed his followers into doing whatever he wanted. He made his dastardly plans seem normal to those who followed his leadership.

And innocent people suffered as a result.

As Dietrich reached the top of the stairs with Serena, Ty expected the doors to slam shut.

Instead, another shadow appeared.

Who was it this time?

As the figure came down the steps—still only a silhouette—Ty suddenly knew that things were about to get much worse for him.

———

CASSIDY STARED AT THE WOMAN STANDING IN FRONT OF her twisting her fingers together with anxiety.

She had dark hair, cut short into a bob. A small, thin build. Pale skin. Uncertain eyes.

Cassidy had seen this woman somewhere before. Only she hadn't looked like this. No, she'd had long blonde hair. No jewelry. Lifeless eyes.

"Rhonda Becker," Cassidy muttered, nearly falling over with surprise. At least, it was the woman formerly known as Rhonda Becker. Cassidy wasn't sure what her current alias was.

The woman glanced behind her, as if afraid someone might have heard. Only Paige and Wes were out there. No one else yet.

Cassidy ushered Rhonda to a seat across from her desk before closing the door. Instead of taking her normal seat behind her desk, Cassidy sat down in the chair beside Rhonda. "Can I get you something? Water? Coffee?"

"Water would be great. Thank you."

Cassidy went to a water cooler in the corner and grabbed a disposable cup. She filled it and handed it to Rhonda, afraid the woman might pass out. She looked anxious—very anxious. Before sitting down again, she grabbed the muffins Wes had brought and put them on a small table between them.

The woman was so thin. When was the last time she'd eaten?

"I've been trying to get in touch with you," Cassidy finally said. She'd managed to track her down and had called several times. She'd finally gotten in touch with the woman's landlord, who'd said she left about a week earlier.

"I know." Rhonda took another long sip, water sloshing out the sides of her cup. She set it down, her hands trembling too much to drink anything. "I was afraid he would find me."

"You were afraid Gerrard would find you? Or should I call him Gilead?"

"He'll always be Gerrard to me." The words looked like they left a sour taste in her mouth as her cheeks puckered and her eyes filled with disgust.

"But you came here," Cassidy continued. "To Lantern Beach. You know your ex-husband is here, right?"

Cassidy was glad she was here, but it had been a risky move, to say the least.

Rhonda nodded, her gaze still appearing dazed and her limbs shaky. "I read the article in the *Raleigh Times*, and I realized exactly what was happening here. I started to do some research, and I knew I couldn't stand by idly anymore. I knew I had to help, if I could. So here I am."

"I appreciate your courage in coming here," Cassidy said. "I know you're risking a lot, but we could really use your help. I'm hoping you can answer some important questions for me."

"I want to do whatever I can to stop my ex-husband from wreaking more havoc." She picked up her cup again and took a long sip. "That's what he does. He destroys things. Destroys people. Yet no one realizes that until the damage is done. They meet him and think he's a gift from God. But deep inside, he's rotten."

Cassidy definitely agreed with her assessment. "I've seen glimpses of that. Why don't you start at the beginning, Rhonda? How did you meet? What happened?"

She seemed to calm herself by drawing in even, purposeful breaths. She looked in the distance for a moment as if being swept back in time before continuing. "We met at Bible college. Gerrard had all the ladies charmed. Everyone wanted to date the man with his bright smile and gorgeous eyes. He was always chosen as the student speaker in chapel because he just had this way with words. Everyone would hang on everything he said. And he said things with such confidence that no one really questioned him."

"I can picture that."

"So when he picked me to date, I couldn't believe it. I felt like the luckiest girl in the world. I was so quiet and insecure. I came from a broken home. My dad left when I was only eight. Gerrard filled these needs in my life that I didn't even realize I had." A certain wistfulness filled her voice as she seemed to remember happier times.

It sounded like Gerrard/Gilead had a radar for broken women he could manipulate.

"What happened then?" Cassidy asked.

"We got married a year later, right after he graduated. I was going into my sophomore year, so I decided to drop out of school to follow my husband to his first ministry. I would be at his side, helping him as needed."

"How'd that go?" Cassidy had a feeling she already knew the answer to that question. Trying not to appear too eager, she took a sip of her coffee and tried to look more relaxed. Nothing about her felt easy-going right now, though. All she could think about was finding Ty.

"At first, it was wonderful. I mean, he was controlling. He liked things the way he liked them, don't get me wrong. Dinner was always at 5:30. He wanted the apartment to be clean when he got home. He liked for me to dress a certain way—long hair, simple clothing, no jewelry."

Cassidy would have guessed that as well. Gilead was controlling and exacting. And Rhonda had probably been easy prey.

"When did things start going south?" Cassidy asked.

"About six months into our marriage," Rhonda started, her eyes looking glazed and her motions stoic. "I got sick—I had the flu. I felt terrible. Gerrard came home, and I didn't have supper ready. The house was a wreck. He accused me of being a lousy wife whom even God would be ashamed of."

"What did he do, Rhonda?" Cassidy tried to brace herself for whatever Rhonda had to say. She could already imagine the scene playing out.

Tears pooled in Rhonda's eyes. Cassidy handed her a tissue and waited as she wiped beneath her eyes.

Finally, Rhonda drew in a shaky breath, ready to continue. "He hit me. Hard. In the stomach. He told me he didn't want to do it, but I had to learn to be respectful to our vows. I was bruised all over—but only in places where no one would see it."

Cassidy swallowed hard. Anthony Gilead was an evil man.

She didn't even want to think about what he might be doing to Ty right now.

But she hoped Rhonda might have some more insight.

CHAPTER TWELVE

MORIAH OPENED HER EYES, her mind still drowsy, her head still spinning, and her vision blurry.

Had this all been a dream? Could she be that lucky?

As her gaze cleared, she glanced around the room.

She was in her apartment. The one she'd shared with Gilead. The one located over the Meeting Place.

Wait . . . maybe all of that really had been a dream.

Moriah tried to move, to jump into action, but she couldn't. A gag had been tied over her mouth. Her arms and legs were bound to a wooden chair. She was trapped . . . again.

How had she even gotten up here? Where had her missing time gone?

That was right. Enoch had injected her with something. Then everything had gone black and she'd passed out.

And now she was here.

She glanced around again, looking for some kind of clue as to what Gilead was planning. There was nothing out of the ordinary that she could see.

Speaking of Gilead . . . where was her husband right now?

Fear shot through her, stark and cold. No matter how she looked at her future, it was bleak. Even if she survived this . . . how would she ever recover?

She wouldn't, she realized. Moriah had made too many mistakes. Too many bad choices.

And now she was going to pay.

Voices in the hallway caught her ear. Someone was talking out there. Two men.

Was one of them Gilead? Was he coming for her?

Another swell of anxiety rose in her.

But the words she heard made her momentarily forget about her fear.

"He's losing it," one of the men said.

Losing it? Were they talking about Gilead? He was the only one who made sense.

"What do you think is going on?" a second man asked.

"Our new recruits are leaving. They said their

lives back on their flooded farms and houses were better than the living conditions here. One even called it 'oppressive' here."

"They didn't sign away their money first?"

"I don't think so. They haven't been here long enough for any insurance payouts to come in."

As they spoke, Moriah tried to work the ropes at her wrists. She considered trying to make noise and get their attention, but she decided to be quiet. No way would they help her. They were all Gilead's minions. They knew she was here and didn't care.

"How are they leaving then?" the first man asked. "They don't have transportation."

"You got me. And then there's the fact that another article came out today in that newspaper. It paints Gilead in a really negative light. I saw him reading it and then he started throwing things around in his office."

"Those articles are blasphemous! I can't blame him." The man paused. "What should we do?"

"I don't know what we can do. I just hope Gilead gets his act together. Otherwise, I'm scared for all of us. He already went ballistic on Kaleb."

"Why did he do that?"

"I'm not sure. I think he overheard him on the phone with someone. He called him Judas."

"If he betrayed us, he deserves to be punished." The man's voice hardened with loyalty.

Kaleb? Would Kaleb have betrayed Gilead? Moriah knew Kaleb's sister had been married to Gilead at one time.

But Kaleb had always seemed so faithful to the Cause. He was a part of the council, along with several others of Gilead's trusted inner circle. Moriah would guess the two men talking in the hallway were also council members. They were the only ones allowed in Gilead's office.

The footsteps left the hallway.

The men were gone, Moriah realized.

But she was still here.

Did those men know she was here? Would they be a part of her demise?

Possibly. And they probably wouldn't bat an eyelash at it. No, they'd do anything for Gilead.

But if Kaleb had broken, then maybe they would also. Maybe Moriah's old mentor, Ruth, would have noticed she was gone. Maybe that woman, however dour she'd been, would try to help. Maybe Moriah would get out of here somehow.

She could hope, at least. But hoping was a big risk, and failure might mean she'd never recover from the emotional fallout.

It also meant she had nothing left to lose.

———

"I WENT TO CHURCH THAT SUNDAY, MY WOUNDS hidden, and I plastered on a smile as Gerrard preached about what a good marriage should be," Rhonda continued, her body hunched over as if in physical pain. "It was horrible."

Cassidy frowned as she pictured it all playing out. She wished she could say she was surprised or that she hadn't seen things like this before. But she had. "I can imagine. What happened at the church?"

"Things were great there for about two years. Everyone loved Gerrard. The church was growing. Then, as Gerrard grew more confident, things started to change. Several people left the congregation and accused Gerrard of preaching things contrary to Scripture."

"Did something predicate the change?"

"Not really. All it takes sometimes is just one influential person who decides they don't like you, and then, Boom! You have a movement on your hands."

"Why did they say they left?" Cassidy asked.

"Because he wasn't preaching the Bible. Honestly, Gerrard never cared about Scripture. He only cared about his own agenda. Maybe a small part of him believed in God and the absolute truth of the Bible.

Maybe. But he cared about his own quest for power more. He just carefully concealed it behind a righteous façade."

"So what happened then, Rhonda? Can you continue?" Cassidy worried about the woman. She just looked so frail right now and emotionally fraught.

She nodded. "As long as you're patient with me."

"Of course."

She drew in another shaky breath. "One of the board members started to look into the church's finances and discovered that some money was missing. The man asked Gerrard about it, and he had some kind of excuse." Rhonda rolled her eyes. "Gerrard *always* had an excuse. He would say he had to buy something for the ministry. Then he would turn things around and make the person who questioned him feel guilty for ever doubting his motives. He was a master at it."

"He's a great manipulator." Cassidy had seen that firsthand.

"But Gerrard finally got in a situation where he couldn't talk his way out of it. Ten thousand dollars went missing. He claimed he had to buy a new vehicle for the ministry so he could visit shut-ins and people in the hospital. But the board said they'd never approved it and he'd violated the terms of his contract with the church."

"And?" Cassidy could hardly wait to hear what happened next. She leaned forward, ignoring the sounds in the lobby. Her crew had obviously arrived, but, thankfully, no one disturbed her.

"True to form, Gerrard had dirt on everyone on the board. He'd probably started collecting it since the very first day he took the job—if not before. He knew things that each of them was ashamed of. One of them had gone bankrupt. Another had a child out of wedlock as a teenager. Another had a son who was a drug addict and in jail for driving under the influence. Because of that, none of them pressed charges against him. No one asked for the money back. They just let Gerrard go quietly on his way, no harm, no foul." Rhonda said the words as if they left a bad taste in her mouth.

Cassidy studied her face. The premature wrinkles. The bags under her eyes. Her limp hair. Rhonda had had a hard life. "And how about you? What was going on in your marriage at this time?"

"The beatings became worse. Gerrard was always sorry afterward, but, again, he had a reason to justify his actions. He was trying to teach me to be submissive. Help me learn what discipline meant. It was awful." She shook her head, more moisture filling her eyes. "The final straw came when he beat me so badly that I lost my baby."

Cassidy sucked in a breath. "You were pregnant?"

"I was." She drew in another shaky breath. "I hadn't told Gerrard yet. I wasn't sure I wanted him to know. I was only eight weeks along—not very far, I know. But it didn't matter. That baby was mine, and I wanted him or her more than I'd ever wanted anything in my entire life."

"I'm so sorry, Rhonda. What did you do after that?"

"I waited one day until he left for work." Her eyes looked empty as she said the words, staring off into the distance. "I'd packed up some clothes, a little bit of food, and a handful of money. I'd put it in a plastic grocery bag, and I hid it beneath some towels in the linen closet. As soon as Gerrard left, so did I. I used my cash to pay for a bus ticket. I wasn't even sure where I was going. I just wanted to go as far as I could."

"Makes sense. I'd do the same." Cassidy had to start a new life also, so she understood some of what the woman had gone through.

"As far as I could go ended up being a little town in the mountains of Pennsylvania. I loved it there. I found a job at this little quilt shop that offered free room and board in the apartment over the store. I changed my look and again started saving whatever money I could. But I was always on the lookout. I used the Internet to try to keep up with what Gerrard was doing."

"What happened? You were living in New Jersey when I called."

"There was one person from the church I kept up with. A friend. Her name was Cathy. On occasion, I'd call her from a pay phone. She told me that Gerrard was gone. She didn't know where. No one at the church had heard from him. I knew the truth. I knew he was probably looking for me." Her face went paler at the words.

"I imagine you were living in terror."

"I was." She glanced at her hands. "Then one day, before I headed down to work, I looked out the window. I saw him. His car pulled up outside the shop. He got out, and I knew he'd found me. I grabbed whatever I could and headed out the back door. I started running, and I didn't stop."

"You were terrified of your husband," Cassidy said, not blaming the woman a bit.

"I was more than terrified. I knew Gerrard would kill me if he found me. Someone from my new church owned a farm. I went there and hid out in the barn for three days. My friend and her husband finally found me between hay bales, and I told them what had happened. They helped me to get away and start a new life. That's when I went to New Jersey."

"You must have thought he'd found you there also?"

"I changed my name and changed my look again. I thought things were going well. For four years, I didn't hear anything about Gerrard. I'd even met a man. A wonderful man who made me feel like a million bucks. I thought maybe I'd have a real chance at happiness." Her momentary smile dipped. "But then I saw one of Gerrard's scouts."

"His scouts?" Cassidy wanted to hear her version of who these "scouts" were and what they did.

"Gerrard has people everywhere, always watching out and doing things for him. I don't know how I knew with such certainty that this man was working for Gerrard, but I just did. It wasn't long after that I got the call from you. I knew without a doubt that something was going on. I got out of town as soon as I could."

"Then what?"

"I figured something was up. I'd kept tabs on Gerrard some. I knew he'd changed his name, and I knew about the cult he'd started. But when I read about the election . . . about everything that had happened here . . . I couldn't just sit on the sidelines anymore. That's all I've been doing, isn't it? I've been hiding while other people have been suffering." Rhonda paused. "What can I do, Chief? I want to stop him. I don't want other people to go through what I have."

Cassidy drew in a deep breath. Maybe this was the lead she'd been looking for.

If she could find something to nab Anthony Gilead on, then she could arrest him.

CHAPTER THIRTEEN

TY BLINKED as the same man who'd hauled Moriah away earlier returned.

He didn't know who the burly man was, but he looked mean with his hard eyes, thick build, and bared teeth.

"What do you want?" Ty tugged against his cuff again.

"I'm checking on you. You can call me Enoch."

"Enoch, huh? What are you doing with Serena, Enoch?"

"None of your business."

The door remained open, affording Ty some light. He could smell rain and hear the pitter-patter of drops on the leaves outside.

He was in the forest. On the island. Soundside.

He made mental notes.

It was gray outside, so it must be daylight now.

"What about Moriah? Where did you guys take her?"

"Also none of your business."

He looked at the man again, a new surge of energy and awareness fueling him. "Enoch, huh? I guess you're one of Gilead's underlings?"

The man grunted. "I'm no one's underling."

"Then why do you act like one?"

Before the question even left Ty's lips, Enoch pulled is arm back and then rammed his fist in Ty's stomach. The air left his lungs as pain coursed through him.

The man was strong. Really strong.

And Ty wasn't in a great condition to fight.

But that didn't mean he wouldn't try.

But not yet.

"Why am I down here?" Ty wasn't going to drop this. He needed as much information as he could get.

He also needed to figure out a way out of here.

Because if Gilead had brought him down here, there was no way Gilead was planning on letting him go. No way. He planned on killing him.

The man nearly growled in front of him before reaching behind him and pulling something out.

Ty sucked in a breath.

Was that a whip?

"I hear you need to pay for your past sins," he said. "The wages of sin is death."

"What sins would they be?" Ty pulled at his chain again.

"Do I need to remind you? How about this? For each one I remind you of, you get another lash from this whip." The man smiled, but the action was empty, void of any true emotion and replaced with mind-numbing evil. All the act served to do was display the brown and yellow stains between the man's teeth.

"I've made a lot of mistakes in my life, but I don't need to confess any of them to you," Ty said.

The man sneered again and raised his whip.

Before he could use it on Ty, Ty grabbed on to the chain above him and used it to hold his body weight. He swung his feet forward and caught the man's neck between his legs.

The man was taken off guard. The whip fell to the ground, and his hands went to Ty's legs. He tried to pry them off.

But it didn't work.

Ty pulled him closer and pressed harder.

The man's eyes bulged. He was losing air.

Soon, he would lose consciousness.

Enoch struggled more until finally, his body went limp. He sank to the ground.

Now Ty needed to figure out how to reach the man's keys and get out of here before Enoch regained consciousness.

———

RHONDA RESTED ON THE COUCH IN CASSIDY'S OFFICE. The woman was tired—she looked like she'd driven all night. Cassidy had brought her some more food and coffee. She'd had a nice meal, and now she was sleeping.

Cassidy had meant it when she said the woman was incredibly brave to come here today. Rhonda Becker was facing her worst fears by being purposefully this close to Gilead. Cassidy had to figure out how to keep the woman safe while she was in town. Their manpower here was already stretched thin, but Cassidy would figure out a way.

As Rhonda slept, the team had met and discussed updates.

Nothing had turned up at the rental houses. The truck that had been pulled out of the Pamlico had been clean with no evidence other than a mark on the side of the door that matched the paint on Ty's vehicle. The phone number that had been used during the call to dispatch to report Ty's accident had been from a burner. No witnesses had come forward.

There was nothing. Still.

But Cassidy was determined not to give up hope.

Cassidy had talked to her contacts with the FBI—Fielding and Easton. They were going to see if they had enough evidence to get an arrest warrant for Anthony Gilead. They were also going to question Melva again and see if she would offer up information on Gilead in exchange for a plea deal. And they were going to ask her what kind of poison she'd used on Ty. It was worth a shot.

Now that all that was over or in progress, Cassidy felt a restlessness stirring inside her again. She wanted to be out there doing something. But she knew the best place she could be right now was here in the office, waiting as information came in.

Paige was doing a surprisingly good job at the front desk, and her years of experience were showing. Wes had left to help in the search, but Cassidy suspected he would be back soon—to check in with Cassidy and maybe even to talk to Paige more.

Colton had asked a few of his friends, along with the men who were scheduled to participate in Hope House, to put their heads together. Colton assured her they were coming up with their plan of action—one that would be off the books and one that it was better if Cassidy didn't know about.

In the meantime, Cassidy had slipped out the

back door. First, she'd grabbed a copy of the *Raleigh Times*. She wanted to read Arianna's article.

She'd climbed into Big Blue. All the broken glass had already been cleaned out, making it safe. She didn't argue when Kujo jumped in beside her.

The sky spit out drops of rain, which plopped on the metal hood and roof. The sound was surprisingly soothing. Ty would enjoy this kind of day.

The thought caused her throat to burn with emotion again.

"Oh, Ty . . ." she muttered.

Kujo nuzzled her neck, and she wrapped her arms around the golden retriever. Kujo missed Ty just as much as she did. Ty should be driving this truck right now, preparing to pick up the guys for a session at Hope House.

He'd been so excited about this next session, about helping other former special forces members get their lives back on track.

Cassidy ran her hand across the dash. And he'd loved this truck. So much of his own recovery after getting back to the States had been spent restoring this classic that had started as a pile of discarded rust. Now, it was beautiful.

She frowned. At least, it had been beautiful, up until this accident.

Shifting her thoughts, she opened the newspaper

and read the new article. Arianna didn't really say anything that Cassidy didn't already know about Anthony Gilead. But there were definitely some incriminating quotes in here—including the one from Cassidy.

I'm not able to speak directly about any ongoing investigations we have here, but I can say that Anthony Gilead is a person of interest. Many people here on the island find his presence to be troubling and are thankful that our local election was rescheduled. I can verify that the county election board is investigating whether or not there was fraud involved.

The back door to the police station opened, and Dane sauntered out.

"Do you have a minute?" he asked. "Or is this a bad time?"

"Climb on in."

After a moment of hesitation, Dane went to the passenger side door, opened it, and slid in beside Kujo. He had a certain awkwardness to him at the moment, almost as if he was about to say something he didn't want to say.

Cassidy only hoped he hadn't come out here to resign. She couldn't handle losing someone else from her office.

"This is probably nothing," Dane started, shifting his weight from one side to the other.

"Let me decide that. What is it?"

"I don't want to accuse anyone unjustly. I know what that's like. But I saw something I thought you should know about. It involves Abbott."

Cassidy's heart pounded harder. "What was it?"

"I drove past Gilead's Cove. I saw Abbott coming from the woods beside the compound. He looked frazzled. And he was alone."

Dane's words washed over her. "You think Abbott works for Anthony Gilead also?"

Dane shrugged, appearing nervous to answer the question. "I don't know. I mean, I never expected that Melva would be working for Anthony Gilead. Who's to say the man doesn't have two people in his pocket?"

"The thought is disturbing, to say the least. Abbott could have been investigating, I suppose." She tried to give the man the benefit of the doubt.

"Maybe. But there was something about the way he walked, the way he looked . . . it was like he was up to something. I just thought you should know, in case it's important."

"Thanks for sharing, Dane." Cassidy let that information sink in. She'd never quite trusted Abbott. She'd hoped her gut instinct was wrong—but what if it wasn't?

"No problem." Dane leveled his gaze. "We're going to find Ty, Chief. We will."

"I hope so."

As soon as Dane left, Cassidy climbed out. She needed to find Abbott and have a little heart–to-heart. Right now.

CHAPTER FOURTEEN

PAIGE AGREED to keep an eye on Rhonda and Kujo at the station while Cassidy went to find Abbott.

The NCSBI agent was still sitting in his car outside Gilead's Cove when Cassidy pulled up, just as Dane had indicated. The man was so deeply involved in a conversation on his phone that he didn't seem to hear Cassidy until she tapped on his rain-drenched window.

He nearly dropped his phone when he looked over and spotted her there.

Guilt flashed on his face as he rolled down his window. "Chief," he sputtered. "What are you doing here?"

"I might ask you the same." Cassidy narrowed her eyes. She didn't even care that she was getting wet or that it had started thundering again in the distance or that the wind had picked up.

No, all that mattered right now was finding answers. If Abbott was hiding something, she wanted to know what. No more games.

"I'm trying to see if I can find out anything more here at Gilead's Cove. I saw a vanload of people leave earlier, and I'm wondering what's going on." He nodded toward the gate in the distance.

"Did you?" A van? Who had been onboard?

If they were headed to the ferry, they would be stopped and checked. Cassidy found reassurance in that fact.

Abbott nodded. "Yeah, I find that suspicious within itself. Who's leaving? Where are they going?"

Cassidy studied his face for another moment and saw a glimpse of his nerves as his gaze wavered. He wasn't telling her the whole truth. "What are you really doing here, Abbott? Who were you talking to just now?"

Abbott flinched in irritation and squeezed his phone tighter. "Just one of my contacts. It's not a big deal."

"You were tromping through the woods earlier right here around Gilead's Cove."

His face reddened, and his eyes narrowed in defense. "Are you spying on me?"

"Nope. But one of my guys saw you. You're hiding something, Abbott, and I want to know what." Any patience that Cassidy had once had for the man had disappeared. She'd given him more than enough chances to come clean.

He let out a long breath and raked a hand over the thinning hair atop his head. "I don't know what you're talking about."

He didn't even sound like he was making an effort to convince her.

"I can get Fielding and Easton in here, if you want." Cassidy wasn't buying his excuse, and he needed to know she meant business.

He may not be threatened by a small-town police chief, but the FBI were the big boys in town.

Abbott's eyes widened. "The FBI? You would bring them in to investigate me? That won't be necessary."

That's what Cassidy thought. The last thing Abbott needed was to get on the FBI's bad side. If he made enough enemies, he might not have a job one day.

She leaned toward him, tired of playing games. "I mean it, Abbott. You've been hiding something since the day we met, and I want to know what it is. I'm not going to be nice about this anymore. You talk, or I do."

He raised his hands and released another defeated sigh. "Okay, okay. I'll tell you. Just . . . calm down."

Cassidy felt far from calming down, but she didn't tell Abbott that. Instead, she waited to hear what the man had to say. And she really hoped he had a good explanation.

"Why don't you get in the car?" Abbott said. "You're getting soaked."

She studied his face one more moment before nodding. Cassidy would get inside his car with him, if only to get out of the rain, which had turned from drizzling to pouring.

But she had her gun with her, and she wasn't afraid to use it.

———

TY'S ARM ACHED, AND HE FEARED HE MIGHT PASS OUT. His fever was high. He could feel it. His muscles ached. His skin was cold but sweaty. His head pounded.

That food poisoning . . . his hadn't been the same as the others. He must have been given a higher dose or a different kind of poison. He could feel it eating away at his body.

He stared at Enoch as the man lay in front of him.

The light from the doorway—though it was gray and rainy outside—offered enough illumination that Ty could finally see everything around him.

Dirty cement walls. Six sets of cuffs and chains. An old crate. Cobwebs. Brittle leaves. A few critters— frogs, if he had to guess.

For the past few minutes, Ty had been trying to reach the keys that had fallen from Enoch's hand when he'd lost consciousness. It was no use. Ty's arm simply wouldn't stretch that far. But he wasn't ready to give up. There had to be another way.

His heavy eyelids tried to pull downward, but Ty fought to remain lucid. Every time he felt himself fading, giving into the fever, he remembered Cassidy. He remembered their future together. Remembered all the plans he'd mentally made.

Plans of staying in Lantern Beach with her forever. Of having children who would run around on the sandy shores. Of teaching his son to fish and his daughter how to change a flat tire.

He had plans for Hope House. Plans to help those who had no one else to help them.

Those plans were just now starting to take form. Though he'd already had one session at Hope House, it had been a soft launch, so to speak. He was just starting to find his footing with his new nonprofit.

And now his friend Colton had come onboard.

He hoped Colton might help him start an offshoot of Hope House—a private security branch to give employment to former special forces members trying to navigate life outside the military.

All those things felt so close.

Ty wasn't going to let Anthony Gilead take it all away from him.

As a new thought hit him, he pulled off one of his boots. With some maneuvering, he managed to get his sock off also. Wasting no more time, he stretched his leg out. Finally, his toes touched the keys.

Ty drew in a deep breath. This might just work.

He stretched forward just an inch more until his toes were able to grip the keys. Carefully, Ty pulled the keyring back toward himself and raised it higher. Finally, he caught them with his free hand.

Hope surged through him, and Ty could taste freedom. If he could just get this cuff off, then he could get out of here . . . providing that his body didn't quit on him.

He reached up and unlocked the cuff. As the mechanism released, he pulled his arm down. Relief swept through him, and he rubbed his wrist. It felt so good to have that thing off.

He glanced around one more time.

He needed to get out of here.

Fast.

Before someone else came to check on him.

CHAPTER FIFTEEN

"SPIT IT OUT, ABBOTT." Cassidy stared at him, her impatience growing with each passing second. Why was he so hesitant to share the truth with her?

Nature seemed to agree. Thunder rumbled, and lightning lit the sky as the rain pounded harder.

"Look, I didn't want to tell you this, but . . ."

"Yes?" She clamped her jaw shut, gritting her teeth, as she employed every ounce of self-control to stop herself from using brute force on the man.

He rubbed his forehead, which was now sweaty. "My nephew joined, okay? Are you happy now?"

Cassidy blanched. "What?"

Had she heard him correctly?

He nodded. "It's true. Dietrich is my nephew."

"Dietrich? The guy who convinced Serena to join?"

Abbott's eyes squeezed shut for a moment, as if demons battled inside him. "Yes, he's the one."

Cassidy threw her hands in the air in exasperation. "Why was that a secret?"

"Because I'm law enforcement. They don't take kindly to having family members who are trouble."

"What do you mean? Everyone has troubled family members. What's the big deal?"

"I mean that, when I applied for this job, I had to list any family members who were felons. I didn't mention him."

"Because you're ashamed?"

Abbott's entire face clamped shut. His eyes. His mouth. Even his nostrils seemed to suck in. "Because I was afraid I wouldn't get the job. I mean, Dietrich is a good kid. And being in a cult isn't a crime. But it's not exactly smiled upon either."

"But you said felon." His story wasn't making sense to her.

Abbott sighed. "Dietrich was heavy into the drug culture as a teen and into college. He was a good kid who got in with the bad crowd. He started dealing drugs and spent some time in jail for it. He's always had some issues. I can't deny that. I never thought he'd do this, though."

Things began to click in place in Cassidy's mind.

"Is that why you keep coming to Lantern Beach? To try and reach Dietrich?"

"Yes, that's why I requested this area be part of my jurisdiction, and that's why I've been spending so much of my time off here on the island. His mom is my sister, and she's been worried sick about him. We'd hoped he would go to rehab. Instead, he joined a cult. I've been trying to contact Dietrich and convince him to get out."

Cassidy's irritation turned to compassion, though she still told herself to keep the man at arm's length. She needed more details before she'd relax around him. "Have you had any luck?"

"No." Abbott frowned, staring out the water-logged window. "Dietrich won't speak to me. The one time I was able to catch him by himself here in town, he told me to leave him alone. He insisted that he knew what he was doing and that nothing would change his mind."

"I see." Cassidy's voice softened as empathy invaded her irritation. "I'm sorry to hear all of this, but I'm still not sure why you wouldn't share that with me earlier."

Abbott wiped his forehead again using a napkin that had been tucked into a pocket in the door. "It's complicated. All I want to do is be a part of the

NCSBI. I don't want anything to ruin it. And I didn't want you or anyone else to use this fact against me."

"You really think I would do that?"

"I know you don't care for me." He narrowed his eyes and let out a snort.

"Only because you were keeping secrets!" If the man had been straight with Cassidy, none of this would have happened.

"I knew how it would look once you knew Dietrich, my nephew, was a part of this group. I knew you wouldn't trust me."

"That's not necessarily true. Your secrets have made me not trust you." She paused. "So, did you talk to Dietrich today? And I thought he didn't live here, but on one of Gilead's other properties."

"He did. Up until yesterday. Everyone cleared out of those other houses that Gilead's Cove owns."

Cassidy blinked in surprise. "What?"

Abbott nodded. "It's true. I have people keeping their eyes on the places. No one has come or gone since Ty disappeared. They're empty."

"That's . . . interesting." What did that mean? She'd think more about it later.

He raised an eyebrow. "Isn't it? I figured he was here. I know he loves nature. I thought for a while that he might become a park ranger or something. I hoped I might catch him walking out near the woods."

"But you didn't?"

"I didn't." Abbott let out a long breath. "Cassidy, I can feel the pressure rising. I need to get Dietrich out before all of this goes down. Just like you want to get your friend Serena out. You know?"

"Yeah, unfortunately, I do know."

Just then, her phone rang. She saw it was Fielding with the FBI. "Excuse me a minute."

She put the phone to her ear, taking care to say the special agent's name. "Fielding, did you find something out for me?"

"I've got good news," he started.

"I could use some good news." She could really, *really* use some.

"I presented the evidence you have on Anthony Gilead to the magistrate, and it wasn't enough for an arrest warrant."

"I thought you said you had good news."

"I do. I kept digging. It turns out, Anthony Gilead cashed a life insurance check for Moriah Roberts's late husband's death. The signature clearly wasn't hers."

Excitement surged in her. "Is that right?"

"Yes, it is. The security camera footage from the

bank clearly shows one Mr. Anthony Gilead/Gerrard Becker cashing the check."

He'd finally slipped up. A surge of joy washed through Cassidy. "That's great news."

"We also checked his banking accounts, and the man is loaded. He's sitting on more than a million dollars."

Disgust rose up inside her. "No doubt that's all from his followers, who give up all their money and material possessions to follow him."

"It's enough for an arrest warrant for the man. Which is exactly what I've got."

Cassidy's breath hitched. "You do?"

"Yes, we've got him, Cassidy. And this case can remain in FBI jurisdiction because of the seriousness of the issues surrounding it. When he goes to court, it will be on federal charges."

"That's the best news I've heard all day."

"I thought it might be. My team is on their way— about an hour out. Keep an eye on the place until we get there, okay?"

"I'd love to."

Maybe—just maybe—Cassidy would get some answers about Ty. She prayed that was the case. Because with every minute that passed, her chances of finding him swept further and further away.

MORIAH COULDN'T JUST SIT HERE, TIED TO A CHAIR IN her apartment with this gag in her mouth. No, surely she'd die if she did.

Instead, she continued to work the ropes at her wrists. She had to get them off. But it didn't feel like the rope was giving, no matter how hard she rubbed.

Her skin was already raw from the cuff that had been attached there. But she didn't care if she had a deep gash by the end of this. A gash would heal. If she died, she was done.

She'd have no chance to make things right.

No chance at redemption.

At the thought of it, Moriah's mind drifted back to her parents. They didn't deserve to suffer because of her actions. She'd already brought her mom and dad so much grief.

She knew they were worried about her for coming here to Gilead's Cove. They'd even talked to Police Chief Cassidy Chambers about her. They'd implored the woman to help them get Moriah out.

If only she'd listened.

But it was too late for that.

Moriah would give anything for some of her mom's chicken and dumplings. To sleep in her warm bed. To have her mama bandage her wounds and tell her everything would be okay.

Why did she have to be so stupid? More moisture welled in her eyes.

She paused as the voices in the hallway drifted through the thin walls again.

Who was it this time? The voice sounded familiar. Was that . . . Dietrich?

"Where's Gilead?" he asked.

"I don't know," another man said. "I haven't seen him. I'm telling you—he's losing it."

"Why? What do you think is going on?"

"I don't think that article in the newspaper helped. It's bad publicity. Gilead feels like it's threatening everything he's worked toward."

"He's got to keep it together. Everyone is starting to talk."

It was becoming chaotic here at the compound, wasn't it? Everything was starting to fall apart. Moriah wasn't sure if that thought brought her joy or fear.

"I'm trying to manage this as best I can. It's not easy. And where's Kaleb? I need his help."

"I don't know where he went," Dietrich said. "He disappeared a little while ago."

"I don't like this."

"Neither do I."

A buzz sounded, and the men quieted for a minute.

"It's the police," Dietrich muttered. "This isn't good."

They must be in Gilead's office, looking at the security cameras there.

"What should we do?"

"I'll take care of Moriah. You warn everyone else."

Panic rose in her. Take care of her? What did that mean?

Before Moriah could think about it too much, the door flew open and Dietrich charged toward her. He pulled her gag off, and his hands began to work the ropes behind her.

"What are you doing?" she rushed, uncertain what was going on and what his plan was.

He quickly untied her, urgency lacing his motions, and pulled her to her feet. He didn't seem to hear her question—or to care. "Do you have a sweater?"

"A sweater?" What was he talking about?

Dietrich jerked her around to face him. "Don't ask questions. Do you have a sweater?"

She pointed across the room. "There should be one in there."

"Get it. Now." He shoved her toward the closet.

With shaky limbs, Moriah did as he told her and pulled on an old blue sweater.

Dietrich examined her arms before offering a satisfied nod. "Good. Make sure your wrists stay covered. Do you understand?"

Her wrists? He didn't want anyone to know what she'd been through. He was trying to protect Gilead still.

Moriah nodded, feeling as if she had no other choice. But anger boiled inside her.

"Some people are going to come." Dietrich got in her face, his voice sharp and quiet. "They're going to ask questions. They're probably going to be looking for Gilead. You know nothing, and nothing has happened, do you understand?"

Moriah nodded again, hearing the seriousness in his voice.

"I mean it, Moriah." His eyes were wide, like he'd gone into panic mode. "Don't try anything. If you do, we have your parents' address."

She sucked in a breath at his words. "My parents?"

"Yes, your parents. I have their address, and I'm not afraid to do what I have to do. Do you understand?" He squeezed her arms so tightly she let out a cry.

Before he could hurt her any more, she nodded.

Fear coursed through her. Dietrich's words made her miss her parents even more. She had to protect them.

"Say it," Dietrich growled. "Do you understand?"

"Yes, I understand. Why are you doing this?"

"I'm trying to hold things together. Wouldn't you do the same?" He took her arm and led her to the door.

She let out a gasp at his intensity. "What do you mean? I didn't do anything."

"He didn't have any of these problems until he married you."

"All of this is happening because Gilead is losing his mind. You and I both know it."

"Don't you dare repeat that to anyone." Dietrich stopped at the top of the stairs. "Here goes nothing. Don't forget what I told you. Your husband told you he was going out of town, but he offered no other details. Understand?"

"Yes, for the third time. I understand."

"Stop back-talking." He raised his hand, about to slap her.

Moriah cowered, covering her face and waiting for the pain.

Her heart pounded in her ears. Pounded. Pounded.

But there was nothing.

She peeked her eyes open.

Dietrich stood in front of her, his eyes wide. He sucked in several shallow breaths as he stared at her. Finally, his hand fell to his side.

"Come on," he said. "Let's go."

Tears rushed to her eyes. Though Dietrich hadn't struck her, Gilead really had created miniature versions of himself.

And that realization left Moriah with only one thought: she would never get away from this place. Never.

CHAPTER SIXTEEN

CASSIDY IGNORED the flutter of nerves that rushed through her as she stepped into Gilead's Cove. The gatekeeper had let the whole team in without any issues.

They were dressed anticipating trouble but not in full tactical gear. No, each wore bulletproof vests and carried weapons. Above them, the sky had turned gray again, and rain had started falling at a steady rhythm. Occasionally, thunder rumbled in the background.

Cassidy had a feeling the full storm wasn't on them yet.

She frowned. Cassidy didn't know how this was going to turn out.

As she stepped down the gravel road, she checked, making sure her gun was locked and loaded. It was. Her muscles were rigid with anticipation.

Fielding and Easton were here, and they'd brought two other FBI agents with them. Abbott had also entered the compound, and Cassidy thought—hoped—they could trust the man.

She'd called in Braden, and he waited at the gate to make sure no one left. Dane monitored the woods around the property, just in case there was a back way out.

Anthony Gilead was not going to get away.

Hope continued to surge in Cassidy. Though she'd searched the property earlier, this was another chance. A chance for confirmation. For more sets of eyes that might see something she hadn't.

"I'm going to take lead," Fielding said, adjusting his FBI vest as they charged toward the Meeting Place. They walked in a group like an army marching to battle. "I'll do the talking once we get inside."

"We'll be right behind you," Cassidy said, thankful she'd been included on this arrest. She'd invested so much time in bringing this man down. Now she wanted to see it happen.

Maybe—just maybe—they would find some answers about Ty in here. She prayed that was the case.

"From the start, I've been afraid that this place

would be another Waco," Fielding continued, his gaze steely and determined as he led the team toward the building in the distance. "We don't want that. We don't want a tactical situation. So let's try to keep this peaceful."

"Roger," Easton said. "Let's go find some answers."

Cassidy's gaze scanned everything around her as they walked through the compound. A few people darted about. As soon as residents spotted law enforcement charging into their space, they ducked back into their RVs.

Strange. This whole place was strange. She'd thought so since the first time she stepped foot here. A body had washed up on the island, and Cassidy suspected the death had ties to Gilead's Cove. From the very first, she'd felt like she'd stepped back into the underbelly of danger, just like she had when she'd lived at the headquarters of DH7, a deadly gang located on the West Coast.

They invaded the Meeting Place, and Fielding announced who they were. Only a few women were in the space, and they froze as they cleaned the tables. No one said anything for a minute.

Finally, movement on the stairs drew their attention. Moriah and Dietrich stepped into the room, looking like royalty among servants.

"Can we help you?" Dietrich asked, straightening his tunic. Everyone else had adopted a plain look, but Dietrich still maintained a trendy vibe, despite his clothes. His blond hair was spiky, his eyelashes thick, and his cheekbones defined.

"We're looking for Anthony Gilead," Fielding said.

Cassidy watched Moriah as she stood beside the man. What was wrong with her? She didn't look like herself. She hadn't since she married Anthony Gilead. But right now, she especially looked pale and shaken. Cassidy had seen the old pictures of her when her mom and dad had come into town and begged for Cassidy's help. Back then, she'd had hope in her eyes.

Was the woman ill? Or just emotionally broken?

"Gilead isn't here right now," Moriah said, her voice weak but her chin high, like she tried to be strong. "Can I help you instead?"

"It's important that we speak with your husband himself," Fielding said. "Where is he?"

"I don't know." Moriah pushed her hair behind her ear. "He didn't tell me."

"He left a few hours ago and didn't tell any of us where he was going," Dietrich added, suspicion flickering in his gaze.

He stood close to Moriah, Cassidy noted. Almost like he was touching her. But he wasn't.

Still, the air between them clearly indicated that Dietrich was dominating Moriah now. Just what had transpired before they came here? Whatever it was, Cassidy didn't like it.

"Did Gilead leave on foot or by car?" Cassidy was determined to find some answers.

"I'm not sure," Dietrich said. "Gilead said he had to take care of some business and left," Dietrich said. "He doesn't have to answer to any of us. Are you sure I can't help you?"

Fielding held up a paper. "We have a warrant for the arrest of Anthony Gilead. We need to find him."

Cassidy continued to watch Moriah. The woman's eyes widened and then lit with . . . satisfaction? Was that it? Moriah had turned against Gilead, hadn't she?

Maybe this was Cassidy's chance to both get information from her and get the woman out of here. She'd been concerned for her safety since the first time they'd met. The woman was lost. She'd made some bad choices. But she didn't deserve this.

"I don't know what to say." Moriah crossed her arms and began rubbing the sleeves of her sweater. "I tried to call him. That's when I realized he left his phone in our room. I have no way of getting in touch."

"Where might he have gone?" Fielding's hands were on his hips, making him look even more imposing than usual. On an interpersonal level, the man was friendly. On a professional level, he was definitely intimidating, and he knew exactly what he was doing.

"We really have no idea." Dietrich sounded crisp and businesslike. Gilead had trained him well. "As I said, he doesn't answer to us."

"I think we'll stick around until he gets back," Fielding said.

"Be our guest." Dietrich extended his hand to the wooden chairs there in the Meeting Place, set in rows facing the stage.

"And we'll need to search the premises first," Fielding continued.

Dietrich looked like he forced a smile. "We have nothing to hide."

Oh, Cassidy would bet they did. This place had so much to hide. The question was: Where were they keeping their secrets?

———

TY DRAGGED EACH FOOT UP AS HE CLIMBED THE STEPS OF

the bunker. Each movement caused a new ache to rush through his body. He never remembered hurting so much.

But he had no choice—he had to push through his pain. Ty had to get out of this place. Before Enoch woke up. Before anyone else came.

Finally, he reached the top of the stairs. He felt like he'd just walked a mile, but it was only twenty-eight steps. He'd counted.

The outdoors greeted him, and Ty drew in a quick breath of fresh air.

Around him, rain fell—it fell hard. The wind felt almost chilly. Or was that from his fever?

He didn't know. It didn't matter right now.

He had to move.

His foot hit the soggy, overcrowded floor of the forest.

Woods surrounded him at every angle. Was this the maritime forest that stretched beside Gilead's Cove? Ty didn't know, but it seemed like a good guess. It made the most sense since Gilead's Cove members seemed to easily come and go.

He paused a moment to get his bearings and figure out which direction to run. The last thing he wanted was to head toward Gilead's Cove.

He glanced at the sky. Without the sun, it was hard to determine east from west. But the door of this bunker would most likely face the water. If that was the case, Ty needed to head south. That would lead him away from danger.

Freedom was almost within his grasp. If he could get out of here, he could find Cassidy. Go to the clinic. Start the recovery process.

And then he would help Moriah and Serena. Those two had to get out of here.

He started to jog away from the bunker. But he'd only made it a few feet when he heard a footfall behind him. He turned, ready to fight down to his last breath.

But, before he could, electricity coursed through him. The shock froze his muscles until he couldn't stand. He collapsed, landing on the soppy ground.

A stun gun. Someone had used a stun gun on him.

He was immobilized. As hard as Ty might want to fight it, he couldn't. The shock had rendered him temporarily useless.

A moan escaped from his lips.

His gaze came into focus, and he saw a man standing over him.

Anthony Gilead.

The man smiled, looking all too pleased with himself as he watched Ty suffer.

"You almost succeeded in escaping." Gilead

sounded unaffected by what he'd just done. "I'm impressed."

Ty wanted to respond. Wanted to fight back.

But he was powerless to do anything until the effects of the stun gun wore off. His fighting instincts wanted to come to life. They roared inside him.

But they were trapped within his frozen muscles.

Gilead grabbed his arm and began dragging him back toward the bunker. "Sorry, Ty Chambers. But I'm not done with you yet."

Despair tried to bite into him.

This had been his chance to escape. He wasn't sure he would have the strength to try again.

CHAPTER SEVENTEEN

WHILE THE REST of the crew split up to search for Gilead, Cassidy remained in the Meeting Place and kept her eyes on Moriah.

Moriah knew something. She was no longer Gilead's little servant.

Cassidy wanted to know what had happened to her and what information the woman might know.

Not only was she concerned for the woman's safety, but Moriah was also her best hope of getting information on Ty.

Dietrich lingered close to Moriah, like he didn't want to give her free reign of the area. They still stood near the stairway as if that was their means of escape if necessary. Both looked stiff and uncomfortable.

Cassidy needed to change that. She walked toward them, determination fueling her every action.

"Moriah, I need a word with you." Cassidy glanced at Dietrich, who stood like a warden beside her. "Privately."

"I'm afraid that's not possible," Dietrich answered for her.

"The woman can speak for herself." Cassidy looked back at Moriah.

The woman swallowed hard, still looking ill at ease. "I don't have anything to say."

"I'll be the judge of that."

"Unless you have a warrant for her arrest, she has no obligation to talk," Dietrich crossed his arms, appearing overly pleased with himself. "Spousal privilege."

"There are two problems with your statement," Cassidy said. "First, spousal privilege only works in court. Second, Moriah isn't legally married to Gilead."

Moriah's eyes widened. "What?"

"That's right. There were never any official documents filed. I checked myself." She'd done so more than a week ago, just in case this very moment presented itself.

"But . . ." Moriah started, her eyelids fluttering with confusion.

"They were married before God," Dietrich hissed. "But I guess you wouldn't understand that."

Cassidy brushed his words off. "I understand what it's like to follow the Bible. I really do. But that's not what this is about."

Dietrich scowled and raised his chin. Cassidy expected him to refuse the interview for Moriah again. But he said nothing.

"What happens if I don't speak with you?" Moriah asked.

"It's your choice," Cassidy said. "But I want to warn you—given the circumstances, I'd hate to see you arrested as an accessory to this crime. I'd want to clear my name if I were you."

"No, you could not charge her as an accessory!" Dietrich snapped, starting to lunge toward Cassidy.

Cassidy raised an eyebrow in defiance, just daring Dietrich to touch her.

Dietrich stared at her another moment before shrinking back and looking away. Finally, he said, "It's her choice. She makes her own decisions."

He probably figured Moriah was better off talking to her here at Gilead's Cove than she would be away from this place. Being out from under the bondage of this place would give her the freedom to speak freely —and to incriminate Gilead without fear.

"I'll talk to you," Moriah said. "But only here, and

only for a few minutes and only in a public spot like this."

"Let's do it, then." Cassidy nodded toward a table set up behind the rows of chairs. "Have a seat."

Dietrich still scowled as Moriah walked away, but he didn't move. The man obviously wanted to remain close. Cassidy would have to choose her words wisely.

The two women sat down across from each other, and Cassidy laced her fingers together in front of her. "When was the last time you saw your husband?"

Moriah licked her lips, still appearing uneasy. "This morning, I think. My schedule has been kind of hectic lately."

"Did he say anything to indicate where he might be going?"

Moriah shook her head. "No, not a thing."

"Did he seem like himself?"

She shrugged. "I suppose. I mean, he's Gilead. He's someone everyone can respect and admire."

"Right. Everyone," Cassidy repeated.

Moriah fidgeted and tugged at her sleeves. As she did, Cassidy glanced down. Was that some kind of wound on the skin there by her wrist? It looked like the skin had been rubbed raw, as if she'd been tied up . . .

Moriah followed her gaze and tugged her sleeve harder until the mark was covered.

Just what had this woman gone through? Could Cassidy ever convince her to leave this place? To run to the safety she offered to her?

Cassidy leaned back, deciding to try a different approach. "How was your trip with Serena?"

Moriah's eyes flickered with uncertainty. "My trip . . . ?"

That's what Cassidy had thought. There hadn't been a trip. Gilead had made that up.

So where had Moriah been? And where was Serena now?

"It . . . it was good," she finally said, wiping a hair behind her ear. "We just went across the water."

"What did you do once you got there?" Cassidy pressed.

Moriah shrugged, her motions still jerky and nervous. "Not much. We had lunch together and did some shopping."

"I'm surprised Gilead allows that."

"He's really much different than you think he is." Moriah glanced up at Cassidy, as if she was trying to communicate something else.

Cassidy got the message loud and clear. Gilead was a monster when he wasn't in the public's eyes. She'd known that since she first met the man.

Cassidy leaned closer and lowered her voice. She didn't care if Dietrich was there listening or not. "Moriah, have you seen my husband, Ty?"

"Ty?" Her voice trembled, and her eyes bore into Cassidy's. "No, I don't think I have. Not since the two of you were here last . . . whenever that was."

"Are you sure? Because I heard a rumor that he might be here somewhere."

"Here?" Her voice cracked, and she touched her throat. "Why would he be?"

"That's what I'd like to know."

She rubbed her throat again, looking edgy but like she tried to conceal it. "He's probably out enjoying a boys' weekend in the woods or something."

A boys' weekend in the woods? What was Moriah trying to tell her? That Ty was in the woods?

But the island had been checked. Even the woods around this place.

"Why don't you go to the police station with me, Moriah?" Cassidy said. "I'd like to do some more questioning."

She had to get this woman away from Dietrich if she was going to get some answers. That was all there was to it.

Moriah's gaze locked with Cassidy's again. "I can't."

What? Why couldn't she? This was her chance to get away. Why would she stay?

Then realization hit Cassidy. They'd threatened Moriah, hadn't they? Cassidy didn't know what leverage was being held over her head, but there was something there. It was the only thing that made sense.

"Are you sure?"

She nodded. "I'm sure."

"Okay, that's enough." Dietrich stepped up to them. "I think you've asked enough questions. Moriah needs a break."

"She can speak for herself," Cassidy said.

Moriah swallowed hard again and stood. "He's right. I am tired. I think I'll wait before I talk to you anymore."

"Moriah—" Cassidy couldn't lose her now. Moriah was the only way she was going to find answers here—answers that could lead to Ty.

Dietrich took her elbow. "She said she's done."

Cassidy drew her gun. "Take your hands off her."

All the air seemed to leave the room. Slowly, Dietrich released her elbow and stepped back. "Okay."

"Chief Chambers," someone said behind her.

It was Fielding. Cassidy recognized his voice. But she didn't alter her position.

"Put the gun down," he said.

"I need to take her to the station," Cassidy said, her gaze still on Moriah. "This man is trying to stop me."

"You know you can't draw your weapon right now. Put the gun away."

Cassidy stared at Moriah another moment. The woman's eyes wavered with unshed tears. She knew something. But what? Cassidy had to find out.

"Chief . . ." Fielding said again.

She held her ground a moment before stepping back. She was letting her emotions get the best of her again. She couldn't do that. As an officer of the law, she knew better.

She lowered her weapon, but her scowl remained.

Fielding was right. If Cassidy did this, it had to be the legal way.

But her heart was breaking inside at the thought. All she could think about was Gilead winning . . . again. And that fact could cost Ty his life.

————

CASSIDY WAS STILL BRISTLY WHEN SHE GOT BACK TO THE police station three hours later. The FBI had set up their headquarters in her conference room and were now conferring there, but she'd slipped away, needing time to herself to process everything.

Gilead hadn't been at the compound. They'd searched everywhere and had found nothing. The FBI had confiscated the man's computer and some other paperwork, where information could be found linking him with insurance fraud.

They'd also talked with Moriah themselves about that insurance check. Moriah had pretended she'd approved her husband to cash it, but it was obvious she was lying.

Easton had told Cassidy he'd seen Serena. He said she wasn't feeling well, but that she'd otherwise seemed okay. She hadn't said anything that sounded any warning bells.

Braden had been left there by the gate to keep guard. When Gilead returned, a whole swarm of officers would arrive to arrest him.

Meanwhile, Cassidy hadn't wasted any time. Rhonda had woken up. Cassidy knew Rhonda couldn't stay here at the station, yet she didn't want the woman to be out and about in Lantern Beach, especially since they didn't know where Anthony Gilead was.

Cassidy got her a room at a local inn and sent Leggott to stand guard outside her door. The arrangement would work for now.

Cassidy had also tried to call Kaleb Walker again. He'd promised to try and get her information, but she still hadn't heard back from him. He hadn't answered, however.

Another dead end.

Everyone here at the station had realized they needed to recalculate everything that was happening and figure out a Plan B. Abbott, Fielding, Easton, and several of their guys were still here and were willing to help with the investigation.

Moriah had said something about woods, so new crews had been sent out to search every wooded lot here on the island.

They were closing the circle. Cassidy felt sure of it.

Still, tension built inside her.

Moriah knew something was wrong. It was like Moriah had been silently trying to send Cassidy a message that Ty was in danger. If only she'd had a few more minutes with the woman . . .

"Hey there," someone said.

She glanced over and saw Mac standing at her office door. He stepped inside and handed her a cup of coffee. She readily took it from him.

"How are you holding up?" he asked.

Cassidy shrugged and took a long sip. "Not well. We're more than twenty-four hours since Ty went missing. You and I both know what that means."

"The crews are out there searching again," he

said. "It's like you told me. Maybe Moriah was giving you a clue."

The conversation flashed back to her, and Cassidy mentally replayed it. "I just want to find him."

"Let's just take this one step at a time. I know it's hard."

"It's more than hard. It's nearly impossible." Cassidy released a long breath, trying not to lose hope.

"Maybe you should go home and get some rest. I know I said it before, but you look like you're ready to crash."

"I can't rest right now. You and I both know that, but thanks for looking out for me."

He plopped down in a seat and nodded for her to follow his lead. "What now?"

She shook her head, wishing she had a good answer, as she sat also. "I don't know."

"The crews have been out there for an hour now. Maybe we'll hear back from one of them soon."

"Let's hope." She leaned down and patted Kujo, who lay at her feet.

Just then, her phone rang, and she saw it was Dane. She put the cell to her ear.

"Hey, what's up?" she said. "Did you find anything?"

"Chief, we have something that you're going to want to see." His voice sounded taut.

"What is it?"

He hesitated. "Can you come to the scene?"

"Of course." Cassidy's guard went up. Something was wrong. What had Dane and his crew found?

Dane rattled off the address.

"That's . . . that's right in front of my home," Cassidy murmured.

"Yes, Chief." Dane's voice sounded soft as he said the words.

Her anxiety ballooned until it was all she could think about.

"I'll be right there." She crammed her phone back into her pocket.

Mac stood and followed her to the door. "I'm coming with you."

Cassidy didn't argue.

CHAPTER EIGHTEEN

CASSIDY AND MAC arrived at the lane leading to Ty and Cassidy's house. A tent had been constructed, crime-scene tape strung, and lights set up to illuminate the scene since darkness was beginning to descend. Rain had started again, and its pitter-patter sounded around them.

Dane and two of Abbott's agents stood there. Dane met them, a strange look in his eyes.

Cassidy braced herself for whatever he was about to show her.

"Chief, we found this body here." Dane hesitated. "I thought you should see it for yourself."

Cassidy walked toward the scene and peered into the ditch there.

She let out a gasp.

It was a body, all right. But it had been burned until it was unrecognizable.

A body . . . of a man.

It's not Ty, she told herself. It couldn't be Ty.

Please don't let this be Ty.

Mac took her elbow again.

"I think it's fresh," Dane said. "You can still smell the fire, you know?"

"He wasn't burned here," Cassidy said. "There would be burn marks on the grass if he had. Someone placed this body here, probably so we'd find it."

She pulled back her emotions. "Anything else about it?"

Dane pointed to the head. "It looks like there may have been a gag on him at one time. You can tell if you look at the back of the head. I didn't move him, but you can see a small piece of fabric back there, as well as a swatch of hair. It looks like the fire mainly affected the front of his body."

Cassidy swallowed hard. "What color hair?"

Dane's apologetic eyes met hers. "Brown."

A gasp escaped before she could stop it.

No, this wasn't Ty. She was going to tell herself that over and over.

"Any other marks that were identifiable?" Mac asked.

Dane leaned down. "Just one really."

"What's that?" Mac asked.

"A wedding ring."

Cassidy's gaze swept down to the man's left hand. Sure enough, a strip of gold was there on his ring finger.

From here, it looked like just a plain gold band that could belong to anyone. The details would tell the whole story.

"Can you take it off?" Cassidy asked, the words nearly sticking in her throat.

"Take it off? Don't you want—"

"Take a picture to document it," Cassidy said. "And then take it off." Her voice left no room for argument. Dane did as she said.

She held her breath until her head swam.

The corpse . . . it was the right size to be Ty. The right hair color.

But this wasn't Ty. It wasn't.

It couldn't be.

After documenting it, Dane reached down and, using a gloved hand, pulled the ring off. Carefully, he handed it to Cassidy.

She could hardly breathe as she grasped it. Holding it to the light, she searched for an inscription inside the band.

As the words "All my love always and forever"

filled her vision, everything went black around Cassidy.

This was Ty's ring. She knew that with life-changing certainty.

———

CASSIDY OPENED HER EYES AND SAT UP WITH A START.

Where was she? Her heart raced as panic tried to seize her.

Slowly, a hospital room came into view.

A hospital room? No, she was at the clinic here on Lantern Beach, she realized.

At once, everything flashed back to her.

The body. Burned beyond recognition.

The ring on his finger.

The inscription on the inside.

A deep sob emerged from her depths, followed by tears.

What was she doing here at the clinic? Cassidy needed to be out in the field looking for clues. Finding Ty's killer.

She grabbed at the IV in her arm. Before she could jerk it out, Mac and Lisa appeared at her bedside with concerned, grief-stricken looks on their faces.

"Don't do that, Cassidy," Mac said, putting his hand over hers to stop her.

She took a few deep breaths, trying to compose herself. "Why am I here?"

"Doc Clemson gave you something to help you calm down. You blacked out and then woke up incohesive. You were saying things that didn't make any sense."

She didn't remember any of that.

"I don't need anything to relax." That sounded like the worst idea ever. She grabbed at the IV again, desperate to get back to work. "I just need to get out of here."

Mac's hand came down on hers again, harder this time. "Calm down a minute."

"I can't calm down. I have to get out of here."

"Cassidy," Lisa started. "You should just try to take it easy a moment."

Something about her friend's words made her freeze.

She knew what Lisa was getting at. There was no rush to find Ty anymore, was there?

Because Ty had been found.

Dead.

Another sob escaped her. She covered her face as a pain greater than she'd ever known welled in her chest.

Lisa pulled her into a hug, her arms firmly wrapping around her.

"I'm so sorry," her friend whispered, "So, so sorry."

"It can't be true." Cassidy's mind seemed a million miles away yet painfully aware of everything around her. "That wasn't Ty's body. It can't be."

"Doc Clemson is examining the body now," Mac said.

But his words sounded grim, like his mind had already been made up.

"What am I going to do?" she whispered. Suddenly, Cassidy didn't care about being strong. About being a leader. No, she just wanted her husband back.

She wanted to turn back time. She wanted to drive Ty home from The Crazy Chefette. Maybe none of this would have happened if she had.

As the thought throbbed inside her, a nurse scurried inside and adjusted something on Cassidy's IV. Silently, she took her blood pressure and listened to her heartbeat. Then she scurried back out.

"We're going to get through this," Lisa whispered. "I don't know how. And I know it's not going to be easy. But we're going to be there for you, Cassidy. I promise. You have a whole lobby of people out there praying for you right now."

The thought of her friends gathering brought her

a small measure of comfort. But it was short-lived as another image of the burned body hit her.

Ty . . . her Ty. They still had so much of life left to do together.

It couldn't be over. Her dreams couldn't be dashed like this.

Because Cassidy's dream had been Ty. She didn't need anything else. Any*one* else.

More tears flowed, and Lisa handed her some tissues.

Cassidy observed Mac for a moment, noticing how he seemed to have aged in front of her. More wrinkles lined his face.

He was taking this loss hard too, wasn't he? Ty had been like a son to him.

Cassidy had to find the person who'd done this to her husband.

She had to find Anthony Gilead.

But her head suddenly felt drowsy. It was the medicine in this IV, wasn't it? Had the nurse upped her dosage?

Cassidy started to reach for the needle taped on top of her hand again. But, before she could, everything faded around her.

CHAPTER NINETEEN

WHEN CASSIDY CAME TO AGAIN, everything felt numb. Dull. Like the events weren't real. Like they'd happened in a movie or in a dream.

She still remembered what had happened. The images wouldn't leave her mind. But the medicine was playing out in her system, making everything feel disjointed.

Lisa still sat in the chair beside her, holding her hand. Mac sat across from her, his head lowered in mourning.

How much time had even passed? How long had she been here? Had she been knocked out?

Cassidy glanced at the window. It was dark outside. She'd guess she'd been there a couple of hours.

More tears pressed at her eyes.

"Can I speak to Clemson?" Cassidy finally asked, needing to get more details from him.

"Of course." Mac stood. "I'll go get him."

Lisa stood by her bed and looked down at her. Her eyes were red-rimmed, and Cassidy could tell she'd been crying also. Her friend smelled like cinnamon, and flour decorated her shirt. She'd dropped everything and come right from the restaurant, hadn't she?

"I can't believe this," Lisa muttered.

"Me neither." This couldn't be reality. It just couldn't.

Cassidy wasn't ready to accept Ty's death as the truth.

Clemson stepped inside the room, Mac tailing behind him. That same grim look captured his face when he saw her.

"Cassidy . . ."

She held back another round of tears when she realized he was about to offer his condolences. "Thanks for coming."

"Of course." He paused by her bed.

"I need you to take me off this medicine."

"Cassidy . . . you passed out. You hadn't slept or really eaten anything. You were dehydrated. Your body was going into shock. I had to do something."

"I know . . . and I know I'm done. Please, Clemson. Get me off this IV. I don't want to numb my pain."

Clemson grimaced and sighed. He didn't say anything for a moment. Finally, he stepped toward her and nodded.

"Okay . . ." He punched in a few things, adjusting the machine by her bedside. "Give it a few minutes. Then I'll get my nurse in here to take the IV out. But you have to promise me you'll take care of yourself."

"I promise," Cassidy said. *Right after I find Ty's killer.*

"We'll keep an eye on her also," Lisa said, nodding at Mac. "She's not getting out of our sight."

Cassidy pretended like she didn't hear Lisa and turned back to Clemson. "That's not the only reason I wanted to see you."

Clemson's eyes crinkled at the edges as he observed her. "What else do you need?"

"Tell me about the body." Cassidy held her breath as she waited for his response.

He grimaced and shook his head, starting to refuse. "Cassidy . . ."

"I need to know. Please, tell me." It was going to be hard. She knew it was. But she was going to have to face the truth eventually. Now seemed as good a time as ever.

He let out a long breath. "It appears to be a male

aged twenty-five to thirty-five. Approximately six feet tall. Dark hair. Good teeth."

So far, all of those things matched Ty's description.

"Keep going," Cassidy said, her heart thrumming in her ears.

Clemson hesitated again. "The time of death was recent—our victim probably died about two hours before we found him. The wounds were fresh. The burns were new."

If only she'd hurried. She should have been out there searching for him herself. Working at the command center had been a waste.

Cassidy could have done so much better, done so much more.

She swallowed back her guilt. "How did he die?"

"It appears he was tied up and set on fire."

"Alive?" Her throat ached as the words left her lips.

Clemson flinched before nodding. "Yes, alive."

Cassidy managed to hold herself together for another moment, but she could feel another wave of despair coming. It built inside her, and she didn't know how long she could fight it.

She swallowed hard. "Go on."

"At this point, the only thing to identity the victim was the wedding ring."

"Ty's wedding ring," Cassidy's said, the words still sounding dead in her ears.

"That's correct."

"But you'll test other things? Like dental records?"

Clemson nodded. "We've already requested those. They should be over by the morning."

She grabbed his hand, desperate for him to hear her next question. "Are you sure it's him, Doc?"

A frown pulled down his lips and he pushed his glasses up, glancing at Mac. "Not 100 percent, Cassidy. But . . . Ty fits the description of this victim."

"What about his shoulder?"

"What about it?"

"He had surgery on it last year. Didn't you have to shave down part of his bone or something? Shouldn't that help in IDing him?"

Clemson's eyes widened. "That's right. I hadn't gotten that far in my examination. I'll check it out now."

"Let me know when you find out, okay?" Cassidy's gaze locked with his.

He nodded somberly. "I will. I promise."

Now Cassidy just had to wait. She needed more confirmation, and she wouldn't rest until she had it.

———

AFTER CLEMSON LEFT, THE MINUTES TICKED BY AT A snail's pace. Cassidy couldn't stand it. She wanted out of this room, but she would wait. Her body needed to lose the effects of the sedative.

"Did the search parties discover anything else?" Cassidy asked Mac, trying to keep her mind occupied. He'd been checking his phone. Maybe he'd gotten a text.

"Not that I've heard." His normal glib tone was gone, and a subtle anger burned in his gaze.

"Where did this murder take place? The place where the body was found was a secondary crime scene. The actual murder took place at a different location. They need to find it."

"Believe me, the police are searching. As soon as they know anything, I'll tell you. The FBI, as well as the NCSBI, are all helping us out on this one. We've got some of the best guys working it."

As Mac said the words, a knock sounded at the door and someone pushed inside. Fielding. He nodded at Cassidy as he paused by her bed.

"I'm so sorry," he said, his head lowered in a respectful manner.

Cassidy only nodded in return.

"I just overheard part of that conversation as I stepped up to the door," he said. "And I wanted to let you know that we did find the site of the murder."

Cassidy held her breath, wanting to hear details but dreading them. "Where was it?"

"In the woods, not far from Gilead's Cove, we found an old bunker."

Cassidy's eyes widened. "Like the one Jack and Juliet were trapped in?"

The bunkers were left over from World War II, back when U-boats had been spotted off North Carolina's shore. Cassidy had only learned of them after another case involving two of her friends back in December.

"I'm not sure of the details of that case, but it was a bunker. Apparently, there's more than one of them here on the island. Inside, we found evidence of a fire . . . and a fight."

She swallowed hard, her limbs starting to tremble "What else?"

"There were some cuffs chained to the wall. It looked like someone had been kept prisoner down there. We're still investigating, trying to figure out all the details. I'll let you know more as I know more."

"Thank you." Cassidy said the words, but they felt like they were coming out of someone else's body.

This couldn't be happening. She just kept waiting to wake up and realize this was all just a terrible, terrible nightmare. Ty would be beside her. They'd go to their screened porch and drink coffee while Kujo frolicked on the beach. Life would be amazingly boring and normal.

Except it wasn't.

Nothing was normal right now.

Someone burst into the room with enough force that the door slammed into the wall.

Cassidy's eyes widened when she saw Doc Clemson there. A new light brightened his eyes as he hurried toward her.

"What is it?" Mac asked.

"Cassidy, I just finished my examination of the body," he rushed. "There's no evidence of shoulder surgery."

"What?" Had she heard him correctly.

Clemson nodded. "It's true. This person who died . . . he'd never had any bone shaved from the joint. Ever."

"But Ty . . ."

He smiled. "That's right. Ty did. This body . . . this isn't Ty Chambers, Cassidy. He's still out there. He's out there somewhere."

CHAPTER TWENTY

TY PULLED HIS EYES OPEN, barely lucid. Agonizingly cold. Teeth chattering. Body aching like it was being destroyed from the inside out.

Anthony Gilead came into focus before blurring again. But not before Ty had seen the man standing over him, that malicious grin on his face.

The effects of the stun gun had long since worn off, but the beating he'd received while immobilized hadn't. That, when combined with his already altered physical state, had left him hardly able to move or defend himself.

And that was exactly what Anthony Gilead wanted.

The door was open behind Gilead, allowing a touch of light inside. Only, it was dark outside. And stormy. Lightning occasionally flashed, illuminating the scenery behind Gilead and making him look even more evil.

"Why?" Ty managed to get out, his voice raspy with pain. "Why are you doing this?"

"You really don't know, do you?" Gilead rubbed his hand, probably sore from throwing punches at an immobilized man.

Ty's vision cleared again, and Gilead came into focus. "I know you were in the Middle East when I was there. You were there at the terrorist compound when we raided it, weren't you?"

"I was." His voice hardened. "Only you rescued someone else."

"We didn't know you were there. Why were you there?"

"I had an incident back here." His face turned stony. "I got angry with someone at the church where I'd been hired. We had words. Words turned into pushes and shoves. He . . . well, he died. It wasn't my fault."

Ty doubted that but said nothing.

"So I did the only logical thing," Gilead continued. "I changed my name and ran away. I needed to come to terms with myself, so I decided to do a pilgrimage. While I was in the Middle East, I began having visions of God's plan for my life."

Ty was pretty sure the man had visions, all right. He highly doubted they were from God.

"I wandered into enemy territory, and I was captured." He scowled. "These men thought I was military. I wasn't. After a year, they finally believed me and allowed me some freedom as their servant."

"And then?"

Gilead crossed his arms, not seeming to be in a hurry. "I learned so much during that time. It was a blessing in some ways. But, of course, I wanted to leave. God had given me this vision of what my ministry would be. I knew I had to come back here."

"How did you escape?"

"These men found some old scrolls. I was fascinated by them. When I had the first opportunity, I slipped away. It wasn't long after the raid where I saw you. While everyone else slept, I snuck out. I took the scrolls with me, as well as some cash that I'd stolen. I can only give credit for my survival to God. I walked for days in the desert. I caught rides."

"How did you manage to get back into the US?"

"Because money talks. That was another lesson I learned. I found a pilot who snuck me back into the country."

"Convenient. But what I don't understand is why no one reported you missing."

"Because I wasn't supposed to be there."

"Why weren't you treated like a prisoner?"

"I was. But their prisoners can graduate on to a new kind of imprisonment. One where I served without food or sleep. They dressed me up so no one could even tell."

"I still don't understand. Why all the revenge on me?"

"Because I saw you. I silently begged for you to rescue me. You didn't even look at me. And then later I saw the articles on you. You were touted as the modern-day GI Joe. The hero. The one who saved the day."

"That's not my doing. The press decided to portray me that way." Ty never thought of himself as a hero—just as someone who tried to do the right thing.

Gilead let out a cynical snort. "I'll agree that you're no hero. What kind of hero would leave a man behind?"

"If I'd seen you there, I wouldn't have done that."

"You didn't even look! You were in charge of the team. You were the one who should have made the call. But you left me there to suffer." He raised the back of his shirt. "And this is what happened."

A maze of scars sliced across his back like spaghetti noodles. Ty looked away. He couldn't imagine what the man had been through. The torture had been enough to make the man crazy, hadn't it?

He'd lost his mind while in captivity. He'd probably had delusions of getting the ultimate revenge.

And now here they were.

"Everything is going so well in your life, isn't it? Meanwhile, I lost everything."

"Look at you now. You have hundreds of followers who worship your every move." An edge of bitterness crept into Ty's voice.

His expression darkened. "They're beginning to turn against me. In part because of that wife of yours."

"She's pretty great, isn't she?" Ty didn't bother to hide the pride he felt for his wife.

Gilead's darkness, his bitter demeanor was replaced with another malicious smile. "She's in mourning right now."

Ty's muscles tightened at his words. "What did you do?"

He shrugged, entirely too smug. "Notice anything missing?"

"What are you talking about?"

"Taking a mental inventory of yourself?"

Ty raced through the possibilities of what Gilead might be referring to. Ty was brought here with only the clothes on his back. There was nothing that could be missing.

Except . . .

He held up his left hand.

His wedding ring. It was gone.

"What have you done, Gilead?"

Gilead smiled again. "I just borrowed your ring."

"To make Cassidy think I was dead?" The thought of it felt like a punch in his gut.

Gilead shrugged. "Something like that. If those are the conclusions she wants to jump to, then that's on her."

Ty fought despair.

More than anything, he wanted to hold his wife. To tell her he was okay.

But, deep down inside him, he wondered if he'd ever be able to do that again. The idea that he might not be able to be with her again broke his heart.

———

CASSIDY FELT A NEW LIFE—AND DETERMINATION— spring inside her as she prepared to step out of her hospital room.

She'd pulled her hair back into a bun and splashed some water on her face, trying to make herself look halfway presentable. The IV was out of her arm, a small bandage on the insertion point. Despite her determination, she still felt pale and weak. Maybe it was the effects of her medication. Maybe she was still reeling from the emotional trauma she'd just been through.

But she didn't feel like herself. No, she felt unsteady.

She braced herself to face the crowds outside her room at the clinic. Though they were all people who cared about her, part of her still felt overwhelmed. All she really wanted to do right now was work on finding Ty. But their loved ones deserved an explanation.

When she stepped into the lobby, a crowd of twenty or so people were there. Most rose to their feet when they spotted her.

Cassidy's heart beat a rhythm of gratitude when she saw their concern and support for her.

Before any of them could offer condolences, she raised her hand and cleared her throat. "I want to thank all of you for coming. It really means a lot to me—more than you can imagine. But I need to tell you something."

Everyone waited silently.

"The body that we found out there isn't Ty," Cassidy finally said.

A gasp went around the room.

"Are you sure?" Austin asked, gripping Skye's hand as they sat side by side.

Cassidy nodded. "Yes, I am. This means that Ty is still out there. And I plan on finding him."

Mac stepped up beside her. "She's telling the truth. I know you're all wondering if she's delirious or on medication. She's not."

"What can we do?" Wes asked. "If Ty's out there, we need to find him. Whoever is behind these acts—and I think we all know who that is—is twisted. Who knows what he's planning next?"

Cassidy turned as someone new stepped into the clinic lobby. Actually, as three new people stepped inside. Three men who all carried themselves like commandos, like quarterbacks in the game of life.

Special forces, Cassidy realized. Then Colton Locke came into view.

"I actually have an idea," Colton said.

"What's your idea?" Cassidy asked. "We're open to anything at this point."

"I called in a few favors, and I was able to borrow a helicopter from a military base not far from here. They're going to let us use their FLIR."

"What's that?" Austin said.

"It's a thermal imaging camera, something that will allow us to see heat signatures. It will allow us to see beyond what's on the surface. We'll search any areas on the island that are dense with foliage and see what we can find."

"I like that idea," Cassidy said. "Let's do it."

He nodded. "No man left behind. That's our mantra. It always had been."

"I want to go with you," Cassidy said. "Is there room?"

"We'll make room for you," Colton said. "But the sooner we leave, the better. There's a break in the weather right now."

"Let's go, then."

CHAPTER TWENTY-ONE

CASSIDY ADJUSTED her headset and yanked on her seatbelt again as the *whomp whomp* of propellers sounded above her. The helicopter had landed on top of the clinic. The roof there had been designed for medevac situations, which were crucial for emergencies here on the island. And that made it perfect for this mission as well.

Though Cassidy had been up in a helicopter before, a brief rush of nerves still swept through her as she anticipated departure.

Darkness had fallen, but Colton assured her it wouldn't make a difference. The FLIR would still work and be effective.

The pilot—he'd been introduced to her as Red—sat in the seat beside her. Colton and two of his guys sat in the back seats. One was Griff, and the other was Brody.

They'd also brought Kujo with them. He wore an official police dog vest as he sat in the back. Cassidy had grabbed one of Ty's shirts so Kujo could pick up on his scent, if it came down to it.

And she prayed it came down to it.

Maybe this was the solution they'd been searching for.

Since this was officially off the books, the FBI hadn't needed to sign off on the mission. But Cassidy had told them what they were doing, and Fielding had given a thumbs-up.

"Everyone ready?" Red asked, his voice ringing through the headset.

"Let's do this," Cassidy said.

Ty, if you're out there, we're going to find you. I promise you that.

No way did she ever want to face another few minutes like the ones she'd had back at the clinic when she'd thought Ty was dead. The dark hole she'd been staring down had been so vast and deep that she still shuddered to think about it. She feared ever going to a place so dark again.

A moment later, Red pulled on the clutch, and the copter began to rise. She sucked in a breath as the earth moved farther and farther away and they glided through the air.

"I think we should head toward Gilead's Cove on the north end of the island," Colton said. "I think it's our best chance of finding him."

"Roger that," the pilot said.

Colton had explained to her how the FLIR worked. She had one, as well as Colton and Griff. They would all be able to use them in the helicopter to search the areas beneath them.

Cassidy pointed the handheld gun-like instrument down below and watched the screen. She could already see little hot spots in the parking lot where Mac and a few others stood, watching them take off.

"We're going to see people," Colton said. "They're going to be outside their homes. In cars. Walking the beach. Ignore them. We're looking for abnormalities."

"I understand."

The *chop chop* of the wings rotating above Cassidy faded into the distance. All she could think about was finding Ty. It was all that mattered.

Please, Lord.

She couldn't stop praying that prayer.

She glanced down and saw lights from houses. She saw tops of trees swaying in the wind. Caught occasional glimpses of water as light hit it.

"How low can you go?" Cassidy asked Red. "Legally speaking."

"Normally, five hundred feet above the surface," Red told her. "In search and rescue scenarios, we're approved to go lower. We just have to be mindful of people's homes and power lines."

"Makes sense."

"What's that?" Cassidy pointed to an area below where a heat signature moved beneath the treetops.

"It's too small to be human. It's probably a deer."

She held back her disappointment, praying that all of this wouldn't be for nothing. This was their best chance of finding Ty. This *had* to work.

Please, Lord.

Cassidy gripped the seat as the helicopter turned, and a rattle shook the edges.

"That's normal," Red said. "No worries."

"Do you see this over here at five o'clock?" Colton's friend, Griff, asked.

Cassidy held her FLIR in the direction he pointed.

She squinted as an orange-colored impression—a heat signature—filled the otherwise dark screen.

Something walked through the woods down there. Another deer? Fox? It was hard to tell.

"Is that a person?" she asked. "Or is it an animal?"

"It appears to be human. Where are we exactly?"

"This should be the woods on the other side of Gilead's Cove," Cassidy said.

"All the search and rescue crews are done in that area, right?" Colton asked.

"That's correct."

"So we have a lone person walking through a maritime forest at night in the rain. I think we're justified in checking that out."

Excitement rose in her. Maybe this would be an actual lead. "I think we are also."

"Think we can land close by?" Cassidy asked.

"I'll make it happen," Red told her.

As he began looking for a place to land, adrenaline surged through Cassidy.

Maybe this was it. Maybe this was her chance for answers.

———

CASSIDY GRIPPED HER FLASHLIGHT AND SWEPT IT ACROSS the ground in front of her.

Red had found a place to land on a sandy beach area just to the west of the woods where they'd seen movement. He'd warned them to hurry, that the weather could turn bad and ground them. He waited in the copter, so they could take off as soon as they got back. Meanwhile, they'd split into two teams and each one had a radio to communicate as well as a FLIR.

Griff and Brody were tracking the figure they'd seen from the air. Colton had stuck with her to search the surrounding area using the FLIR. Cassidy had Kujo on a leash, ready to utilize the dog's skills.

She held Ty's shirt up to Kujo's face. "Find him, boy. Can you find him?"

Kujo sniffed the shirt and then turned his nose in the air, as if trying to pick up a scent. Finally, he seemed to hone in on something. He tugged the leash toward the forest.

"Let's go," Colton said.

They took off with the dog. Cassidy dodged trees and saplings and underbrush as she let Kujo take the lead. Branches scratched her legs, but she didn't care. All that mattered was keeping up with Kujo.

"He's definitely caught the scent of something," Colton said, moving easily beside her.

"Let's hope this leads us to Ty."

Colton's radio crackled and he spoke into it. Cassidy couldn't make out what was being said.

"Updates?" she asked, breathless as she tried to keep up with Kujo and avoid the tangle of prickly vines. Time was ticking away. She heard thunder in the distance again as the temperamental weather reared its head. The storm just needed to hold off for a little while longer.

"Griff saw someone running toward the fenced-in area of Gilead's Cove, but they lost him."

"Are they jumping the fence?"

"It's your call. What do you say?" Colton glanced at her.

"I don't have a warrant. I can't authorize it." She paused. "But I won't tell them no either."

Colton smiled in an "atta girl" manner. "I'll let them know."

Kujo stopped in the middle of the woods and barked at a patch of underbrush. Cassidy dropped his leash and shone her flashlight in the area. It was a patch of briars . . . or was it?

Colton dropped to the ground and began moving the underbrush away with his hands. He paused. "It's a door, Cassidy."

"A door?" She leaned closer and sucked in a breath as realization hit her. "It's another bunker."

"Let me get this open." Colton tugged at the handle, but nothing happened. "There's a lock over the handles. . . I need something to break it."

Kujo barked at the door.

Ty was in there, wasn't he?

Cassidy could hardly breathe as she thought about it.

They had to get to him. Her gut told her they didn't have any time to waste.

"Maybe the pilot has something in the copter," Cassidy said.

"Let me radio him and find out." Colton put his radio to his mouth, said something, and then turned back toward her. "Red is bringing a bolt cutter with him. Hold tight."

Cassidy could hardly wait. No, she wanted inside that bunker. Now.

So did Kujo. The dog continually barked at the doors.

Cassidy got on her knees and pounded at the metal door, one that was probably seventy or eighty years old. "Ty, are you in there?"

She put her ear closer, listening, hoping to hear a sign of life.

Nothing.

What did that mean?

She pounded again. "Ty?"

Nothing.

"He could be gagged," Colton said.

That was right. Gagged. That was probably it.

Cassidy pushed aside the worst-case scenarios. They weren't going to happen. No way.

Focus on the solution, not the problem. Cassidy could hear Ty telling her that.

Red ran through the woods with a bolt cutter in his hands. He shoved them aside and went to work on the lock. A moment later, it snapped in half.

Colton tossed the broken latch aside and then threw open the doors.

Before Cassidy could stop him, Kujo raced down the stairs. Cassidy stayed on his heels, her thoughts suspended in time, in anticipation.

The beam of her flashlight hit on something on the floor.

Someone on the floor.

"Ty . . ." Cassidy dropped to her knees beside him, a cry escaping from deep inside.

He . . . he wasn't moving.

No!

Colton knelt beside her and put a finger on Ty's neck. "He's got a heartbeat, but he's going to need some medical help. Soon."

What had Gilead done to him? Bruises battered his body. His face was swollen. He moaned beneath his breath.

He was on death's doorstep, she realized.

"Come on, Red," Colton yelled. "Let's get him back to the copter."

Cassidy moved out of the way as Colton threw Ty over his shoulder. Wasting no time, he hurried up the steps and through the forest. Kujo and Cassidy stayed on his heel.

As they rushed, Cassidy spotted lightning in the distance.

Lightning?

No, they couldn't be grounded. Every moment mattered right now. If they were stuck here, they'd never get Ty the help he needed in time.

They'd found him, though. They'd really found him.

But Ty wasn't out of the woods yet.

They reached the copter, and Red motioned for them to hurry as they climbed inside. Griff and Brody appeared at the same time, running from the woods. Red had radioed them when they found Ty.

More lightning flashed offshore.

The storm was close.

Really close.

They all climbed inside and adjusted Ty in the back seat. Colton and Griff knelt on the floor beside him, and Colton put an oxygen mask over Ty's mouth. The man had paramedic certification as part of his SEAL training.

"We've got to go," Red said. "Now."

Cassidy pulled on her seatbelt and prayed for the best.

CHAPTER TWENTY-TWO

CASSIDY PACED the hallway of the Lantern Beach medical clinic. Doc Clemson was in the room with Ty, examining him and treating him.

But she hadn't heard any updates. Didn't know the status of his injuries.

Not yet.

They'd talked about taking him to Raleigh via helicopter since the city had a more comprehensive medical center. But Ty's fever was so high, Colton said they needed to get it down first—and fast. There wasn't time to take him into Raleigh.

Her friends had gathered again, and Cassidy was incredibly grateful for their support. Several people tried to talk to her in the waiting room, but she didn't feel like answering questions. In fact, she barely heard them.

Instead, she'd heard other things that had been muttered.

Septic.

Broken ribs.

Concussion.

Dehydrated.

Poison still in body.

None of those things could be good.

"He's a fighter, Cassidy." Colton stopped in front of her. "He's going to pull through this."

She nodded, trying to register his words. "He is a fighter. But I never thought I'd see him like we did. He looked . . . bad. So bad."

"He did look bad. But he's still alive. You have everyone praying for you two in there."

That meant the world to her, but . . . "I need to find the person who's responsible for this."

"I know. You will. Give it time. The important thing now is that Ty has been found."

She couldn't argue. He was absolutely correct. "Thanks for all your help, Colton. I really do appreciate it."

He nodded solemnly, humbly. "Ty would have given up his life for me. This is the least I can do for him."

Cassidy paced a few more minutes, trying to make sense of her thoughts. To sort through everything that had happened.

She needed a moment alone, and there was only one place she could think to go to get that.

"Listen, Colton," she started. "I'm going to go to the chapel for a minute. If anyone needs me . . ."

"Take all the time you need. But I'll make sure someone gets you if the doctor comes out."

"Thank you."

She needed to have a long talk with God.

She walked down the hallway and turned down a short corridor that ended at the chapel. The space was the size of a patient's room at the clinic. Three short pews were on each side and a stained-glass window graced the front of the room. A Bible was on display in front of it.

One of the local churches had just paid to convert an unused office here into the space. Cassidy had gotten a sneak peek of the room several days ago.

Cassidy stepped inside the dark space, surprised no lights were on. Just as she reached for the switch, she heard a sound.

"I wouldn't touch that if I were you," a deep voice said.

She froze.

Then she reached for the light switch anyway.

"Don't do that," the voice said. "I have a gun

pointed at you. If you touch that switch, I'll use it and end it all right now."

That's when Cassidy realized who the voice belonged to.

Anthony Gilead.

He was here. At the clinic. In the chapel. With Cassidy.

———

CASSIDY REACHED FOR HER GUN BUT STOPPED HERSELF. Gilead seemed to have a better view of her than she did of him.

And when he threatened to use his gun, she had no doubt he was telling the truth. The man had nothing to lose at this point.

"Reach behind you," he said. "Lock the door."

Cassidy swallowed hard, wondering if she should run. But he'd shoot her if she did. Instead, Cassidy did as he asked.

"Hand me your gun," he continued. "Actually, put it on the floor and slide it away from you, toward the sound of my voice."

Cassidy's stomach clenched, but she did as he asked. Now she was totally helpless and at the man's mercy.

"What are you doing here?" Her lungs froze

along with the rest of her body. She couldn't risk a wrong move.

If only she could see the man. Could see what he was doing.

But she couldn't. All Cassidy could do right now was remain still.

"You found him," Gilead said, his voice holding surprise and maybe outrage.

He was talking about Ty. Gilead had thought he was smarter than everyone else. He hadn't seen this coming, had he? He'd never thought Ty would be discovered. Nor did he ever think he would be charged with this crime.

"I did find him," Cassidy said.

"Kudos to you. I figured the other dead body would only throw you off for a while. I thought the wedding ring was a nice touch."

"You forgot about his shoulder surgery. The bones told the truth."

"Like I said, I was only buying some time and enjoying myself as I watched you suffer. I knew as soon as the dental records came in, you'd discover the truth. But that would be plenty of time for you to suffer."

More anger burned through her.

"You nearly did kill Ty. I don't know how you

could do that to him." Cassidy's voice sounded just above a growl. "He's done nothing to you."

"Ty knows about his sins. We had a long talk."

His sins? Gilead must be talking about the incident in the Middle East that Ty had told her about before he'd gone missing. Gilead must have developed some kind of rage inside him against Ty after the event.

"He didn't purposefully leave you behind in the Middle East, you know." Cassidy clenched and unclenched her hands. The man was delusional.

"He certainly didn't try to help."

"Whose dead body was that left out in the woods with Ty's ring on his finger?" Gilead had planted that person there so Cassidy could think it was Ty. He truly was heartless . . . maybe even diabolical.

"Hmm . . . that's a good question, isn't it?" Amusement rang through his voice. "Let's just say it was someone who died to me. Someone I found out was working with the police to bring me down. At least, he was planning to do that."

Cassidy sucked in a breath. "Kaleb?"

"You should have never contacted him. We saw his phone history. We can't have any traitors at Gilead's Cove."

Cassidy swallowed hard, pushing away more

guilt. Maybe she shouldn't have called the man. She'd have to deal with that later.

Right now, she had a killer standing in front of her. "You still haven't answered my original question. What are you doing here?"

"You and I need to have a little talk. Just you and me. No one else. This was the only way I could do it."

"So here we are. Talk." *Breathe in, Cassidy. Breathe out. Stay calm. Emotions will only get you in trouble.*

More of Ty's advice.

"I need to make a little deal with you."

"I'm not fond of the idea of making any kind of deal with you." It would be like making a deal with the devil. But she really was curious about where he was going with this.

"You'll want to hear these details," Gilead crooned.

"Then tell me." Cassidy's spine pinched with irritation. This was all about playing his games again. He would do anything to keep the upper hand.

She needed to make him believe he had it.

"I know your little secret, Cassidy."

She sucked in a deep breath as she remembered the mysterious texts she'd received from someone who'd threatened to reveal her real identity. Doing that would make it unsafe to live here in Lantern

Beach. Would mean she'd need to run. Change her name again. Her look.

"I don't know what secret you're talking about," she said.

"I'm sorry, maybe I should have said *Cady Matthews*."

So it was Gilead. He was the one who knew. Cassidy sucked in a breath.

"Tell me about this Cady Matthews." Cassidy tried to buy time. Maybe someone would come in. Help her out here. But she didn't dare make a move. Even though she couldn't see Gilead's gun, it was like she could feel that it was aimed right at her.

"Oh, let's see. She became like an urban legend. Some people even made cartoons of her. She went undercover, killed a gang leader, and helped the oppressed members and victims finally find a life again. There was a million-dollar bounty on her head, but she died before anyone could cash in. Case closed. Danger absolved."

"Sounds like an interesting story. I'm not sure why you think it's connected to me."

He chuckled before clucking his tongue as if humored. "I think you do, Cady. We just need to figure out what we're going to do about it."

"What are you talking about?" Cassidy's eyes had adjusted to the darkness, and she could barely make out the outline of the man, standing only a few feet in front of her. How had he even gotten in here without being seen?

Maybe because everyone had been so distracted with Ty. No one thought Gilead would be this brave or emboldened. Not even Cassidy.

"I won't tell your secret if you won't tell mine," Gilead said in a singsong voice.

"What secret are you talking about?" Cassidy wasn't going to give up any more information than she had to. Gilead was going to have to lay out these details himself. She wouldn't make it easier for him.

"You don't press charges against me. You bury this little incident. And I'll keep your secret safe."

Outrage pummeled through her. He was trying to formulate a plan to get away with what he'd done. "Wait, you want me to pretend like you didn't abduct and nearly kill my husband?"

"A life for a life. You know if I share what I know about you with the world that life as you know it will be done. So if I lose my freedom, so do you."

A buzz hummed in her ear. "You need to pay for what you did."

"Cady, need I remind you that you took a life? You're not innocent."

She was careful to keep her tones even. He was trying to shake her up, but it wasn't going to work.

She had taken a life, but it had been an accident and as an act of self-defense.

"I don't know what you're talking about," she said. "But I do know that you're not innocent."

"Or am I?"

"You expect me to believe that you didn't have anything to do with any of these murders here on the island? I know you covered your tracks and tried to make it look like your hands were clean. But you're not fooling me. You have your hand in everything."

"I don't know what you're talking about." He sounded smug, like he was so wrapped in the delusion that he was untouchable, that he honestly didn't believe he could be caught.

Cassidy's muscles clenched. She wanted more than anything to smack the man. To do worse than that, if she were honest with herself.

But she held herself in check. For Ty's sake. She'd be no good to anyone if she was dead.

"Is it a deal?" Gilead crooned.

"No, it's not a deal," Cassidy snapped.

"One wrong move on your part, and the world will know your news. Just keep that in mind."

"You're one lousy, no good, arrogant—"

Before she could finish her sentence, someone pounded on the door behind her. "Cassidy!"

Acting quickly, she reached back and flipped the

lock. Two seconds later, she hit the switch, and light filled the room.

Just in time to see Gilead running toward the back of the room.

"Cassidy, Ty is awake," Dane said. "Colton sent me to come get you."

"Ty?" She swung her head back around to Gilead just in time to see him escaping out the emergency exit door. "Dane, it's Gilead. You've got to catch him."

Dane's eyes widened for just a second, and then he took off after Gilead.

She was going to have to trust Dane to catch him.

Because right now she needed to see her husband. See with her own eyes that he was okay.

Gilead was going to have to wait.

CHAPTER TWENTY-THREE

CASSIDY RUSHED into Ty's room, brushing by Doc Clemson and his nurse as she darted to Ty's bedside. She needed to see him for herself. Needed to see he would recover.

She paused there and stared at her husband.

Oh, Ty . . .

He looked so battered and bruised. His eyes were swollen and closed. Dark blotches stained his face. An oxygen tube was in his nose and an IV in his arm.

"I'm sorry, Cassidy." Clemson's quiet voice stretched through the room as he stood near the door. "He woke up for a moment but then faded again. His body has been through a lot over the past couple days. He needs to rest."

"Is he going to be okay?" She grabbed Ty's hand

and squeezed it, hoping that would somehow let him know she was here.

"We finally got his fever going down," Clemson said. "I'm pumping antibiotics into him. He has a broken rib. A busted lip. Possibly a sprained wrist. He's dehydrated, and we're trying to figure out what was used to poison him by doing some lab work. According to the FBI, Melva refused to give up any information on it. But I think Ty is going to pull through this, Cassidy. We just need to give him some time."

Relief washed through her. *Thank You, Jesus!*

"How long will he be out?"

Clemson glanced at Ty. "It's really hard to say. But he needs to sleep in order to heal. Let's give him a few hours."

Cassidy nodded. "Can I have a minute alone with him?"

"Absolutely. Take all the time you need."

As Clemson and his nurse left, Cassidy leaned toward Ty. A new round of tears rushed to her eyes. She didn't even know she could produce this many tears. She wasn't generally an emotional person. But this situation . . . it had definitely turned her world upside down.

She kissed Ty's cheek, absorbing the features of his familiar face. His thick brown hair that he wore brushed out of his eyes. His high cheekbones. Thick eyelashes.

He was perfect for her in so many ways. He'd carried her through some of the hardest times of her life. She would be here for him now. Forever.

You keep my secret, and I'll keep yours.

Gilead's words echoed in her ears, causing a fresh round of anger to heat her veins.

There was no way she could let Gilead get away with doing this.

No way.

Cassidy didn't care if her name was on every hit list out there. She wasn't going to let him walk.

She was also certain that Ty wouldn't want her to do that either.

"I'm going to get Anthony Gilead," she whispered to Ty. "When you wake up, this is all going to be over."

She kissed his cheek one more time before stepping back, a new resolve tightening her spine.

She needed to meet with her guys. Now.

It was time to end all of this for good.

———

"WAIT," MAC SAID. "ANTHONY GILEAD WAS HERE? IN the clinic?"

Cassidy paced the chapel area, looking for any clues the man might have left. There was nothing. Fielding and Abbott had joined her in the space so she could update them as well. Dane had also joined them, while Easton remained in the bunker, investigating the crime scene there.

"That's right," Cassidy said. "He took my gun and threatened me if I made any noise or made any moves. He ran before I could apprehend him."

She glanced at Dane, waiting for him to fill in any more details.

"He had a car waiting outside," Dane explained. "He jumped in, and they took off. They were gone before I could get to my patrol car."

"What did he say?" Fielding asked.

She remembered his threat one more time. He was not going to have this power over her, though. "He admitted to doing this to Ty, and he also admitted to killing Kaleb Walker."

"Who's Kaleb?" Fielding asked.

"He's the man we found burned to death on the side of the road, the one who wore Ty's wedding ring. He was a member of Gilead's Cove."

"We need to arrest this guy," Fielding said, his jaw tightening.

"I agree." Abbott straightened. "This has just

reached a new level of horrible. This man is in way deeper than just insurance fraud."

"We need to assemble a team," Fielding continued. "It sounds like this guy is completely losing it. I don't think he's going to take kindly to us going into his compound again."

"I don't think so either," Cassidy said. "Something tells me he's gearing up for a fight. So what's our plan?"

"Give us an hour." Fielding glanced at his watch. "And then we're going to move in. We're going to take this guy down."

"Got it," Cassidy said. "Let's meet back at the police station then."

As everyone walked away, Mac remained.

"How is Ty?" Mac asked.

"I think he's going to be okay. He's really beat up. But . . . he's going to pull through. I can just feel it."

A grin lit Mac's face. "I'm so glad."

Mac pulled her into a fatherly hug.

"What else did Anthony Gilead say, Cassidy?" Mac asked as they stepped away from each other.

She hesitated a moment. "He's the one who sent me those texts, Mac."

"Gilead knows who you really are? How?"

"My guess is that as he was doing research on Ty, he probably discovered information about me. He threatened to reveal who I really am if I push forward with this case."

"Yet you're pushing forward anyway?"

"I'm not going to let him dictate what I do and don't do."

Mac nodded before a grin tugged at his lips. "That's my girl. But I'm not sure what this is going to mean for you."

"I don't know either. But I've just got to trust God with this. He knows everything that's going to happen. He's going to provide a way for me too."

"Let's get going then. We have a big night ahead of us."

"And I want to be here for Ty when he wakes up."

"Then we don't have any time to waste."

CHAPTER TWENTY-FOUR

MORIAH FELT stiff as she stood on the stage beside Gilead.

He'd returned to the compound, had stormed up to their apartment—where Dietrich had left her tied up again after the police left—and he'd demanded Moriah comply with him or else he'd hurt her family.

She was trapped. There was nothing she could do. She couldn't risk her parents' lives. They were good people. And all she'd ever been was selfish.

Not anymore.

So when Gilead led her downstairs to stand beside him on stage as he hosted a special meeting in the middle of the night, Moriah had no choice but to remain beside him.

There was no one here who would help her. They were all followers of this man. Believers in his supposed book of the Bible, Makir. Moriah would never be able to convince these people otherwise.

But calling a meeting at this hour was strange, even for Gilead. What was going on?

Everyone else looked just as confused as Moriah felt. They whispered. Wiped sleep from their eyes. Glanced around, as if looking for answers.

She glanced across the room as Ruth stepped into the back. Ruth, the woman who'd once been her mentor. Funny, at one time she'd looked so homely. Right now, her shoulders were back and her chin high, like she had a personal stake in this.

What was going on?

"Everyone, thank you for meeting here on such short notice," Gilead started from behind the pulpit.

Moriah jerked her gaze back to him. He didn't look like himself. His motions were jerky. His eyes were bloodshot. What was going on with him? Even his clothes looked rumpled, maybe like he'd been out in the rain.

Whatever was going on here, it was bad.

Gilead wasn't in his right mind.

"We've come here together tonight for a special communion service," Gilead continued.

Communion service? They'd never had one of these before. Why now?

"Communion is a special time of coming before

God and honoring everything He has done in our lives," Gilead continued. "It's a time to think about sacrifice . . ."

Moriah tuned him out and glanced across the room again. This time she spotted Serena sitting in the back with Dietrich beside her. She looked just as scared and confused as Moriah felt.

As did the other two hundred or so people here.

Moriah had heard that a vanload of fifteen people had left the day before and that there were others who wanted to leave. Maybe people were finally starting to see through Gilead. Did she even dare hope? That might explain his behavior right now.

"We're going to hand out these communion cups now," Gilead said. "And the bread. Please hold them as they're passed. We're all going to partake at once."

His men started passing around silver trays with bread and cups of juice. As they moved, Moriah spotted the guns tucked into their waistbands.

Gilead began talking about the importance of breaking bread together. Started quoting from Makir.

Moriah barely heard him. She just needed to figure out his end game.

What was her husband up to right now?

She glanced around the back of the room. Another set of Gilead's men stood there.

The council, she realized.

Members of the council stood at the edge of the room, almost like they were on guard.

They were, weren't they? Something was going down tonight.

And it had something to do with this juice and bread.

A bad feeling grew in her stomach.

———

CASSIDY BRACED HERSELF AS SHE AND THE OTHER LAW enforcement officials surrounded Gilead's Cove. She had a feeling this wouldn't go well. Fielding obviously didn't think so either. Why else would they all be wearing full tactical gear?

Fielding and Easton were here along with three other FBI agents. Abbott also had three NCSBI agents with him. Cassidy had brought Dane and Braden with her. They were a small team, but Cassidy hoped they could make this work.

Colton and his Navy SEAL friends had wanted to come along, but Fielding had refused since they weren't officially law enforcement.

Meanwhile, Mac had stayed with Ty. Someone needed to keep an eye on him, just in case. Leggott was still at the inn, watching over Rhonda Becker until this storm passed.

Fielding gave them instructions as they gathered outside the compound. They were only after Gilead. No innocent civilians were to be harmed.

"You guys," Abbott said, staring at his phone. "I just got a report on one of the people who's a part of Gilead's Cove. Her name is Ruth Merlinger. Apparently, she used to work as a chemist for poison control."

Poison control? Cassidy hadn't seen that coming.

She remembered meeting Ruth. The woman had hovered around Moriah on several occasions when Cassidy had been there. She'd seemed overbearing and watchful.

Despite her downcast and unassuming appearance, she'd apparently just been another of Gilead's minions.

"Given the fact that this group has a history with the hallucinogenic drug flakka, salmonella, and oleander, I have to wonder if this woman was the mastermind behind it," Abbott continued.

"We would have found a lab, wouldn't we?" Cassidy asked. "We've checked all of Gilead's properties here on the island."

"But what we didn't know was that this group owned a boat down at the marina," Abbott continued. "It was in Ruth's name, so it didn't register for us during any of our searches. One of my guys is there checking it now."

"Why didn't I even know you were looking into this Ruth woman?" Cassidy asked.

"You were a little preoccupied with Ty," Fielding said. "One of my guys was doing surveillance on this compound earlier and took a picture of her. We ran the photo through a computer search and found a match."

"She's in your system?" Cassidy asked, surprise lacing her voice.

"That's right. She killed her husband and then disappeared. This is the first time she's shown up on our radar since then."

Cassidy shook her head, trying to stay focused. "What did your guys find when they went on Ruth's boat?"

"They found a lab and said she was making some kind of concoction. Said it looks almost like juice. And they have all these old boxes that computer paper came in. They probably transported this to the island in those boxes."

"I saw those boxes in Gilead's closet," Cassidy said. "I didn't think to look inside them."

"Neither did I," said Fielding. "This is worse than I thought."

He could say that again. Gilead was going to

poison everyone here, wasn't he? That was his end goal—or at least his backup plan if things got too precarious.

Which was exactly what was happening right now.

They didn't bother to ring the bell at the gate. Instead, on the count of three, they all scaled the fence that surrounded the compound. They quietly moved toward the Meeting Place together. Even from the distance, she could see the lights were on.

Were people in there?

She had no idea.

But this raid was going to take the community by surprise. It had to be this way if they wanted to catch Anthony Gilead.

"Move forward," Fielding said into their coms.

Like trained soldiers, they all did as he said. They were going to close in and give Gilead nowhere else to go.

Anger still burned through Cassidy at the thought of what he'd done to Ty. This man deserved to pay. He needed to be stopped.

And this was the only way that was going to happen.

"Anyone see any signs of movement?" Fielding asked.

"Negative," someone else said.

Good. Maybe this would be easier than she thought.

But that rarely happened. She knew that just as well as anyone.

Cassidy took another step when she heard a bullet whiz by.

She ducked, searching for the gunman.

Then more bullets came. And more. And more.

Gilead had watchmen waiting for them.

And they were shooting to kill.

Things had just gotten one hundred times more precarious.

CHAPTER TWENTY-FIVE

MORIAH'S HEART raced faster and faster.

Something was wrong. Majorly wrong.

She jumped at the sound of something cracking through the air outside. It was too brief to be thunder. Too loud to have been something that had fallen.

It sounded again and again.

Moriah knew the truth . . . she just didn't want to face it.

Those sounds had been bullets.

Her heart pounded in her ears.

Everyone else must have heard them also. Heads began swinging around. A murmur shuffled through the room.

Were the people inside this room being shot at? Or were Gilead's people taking fire at someone else? Was that why they'd been called here?

"Calm down, everyone." Gilead's hands gripped his wooden podium. "We've got this situation under control. The Bible says that people will hate us for the Cause. This is just another example of people hating us because of what we believe. We need to stay strong, even when people turn against us."

People quieted but still held on to each other. Fear stretched across their gazes.

Then another round of bullets sounded.

Gilead's face reddened. "Those bullets are the sound of freedom. Of protection. They're being fired because there are people out there who want to hurt us. Who want to persecute us. We can't let that happen. We must defend ourselves."

A tremble raked through Moriah. This wasn't going to be good. Now, everything was coming to a head in the worst way possible.

"We need to stand strong," Gilead continued, his voice rising above the murmur of the crowd. "God gave me a vision. He showed me what tonight would look like, and that was one of the reasons I called you all here. So we could be safe together. So we could pray together. So we could commune together. God will protect us, just like He protected Daniel in the lion's den. Like He protected Shadrach, Meshach, and Abednego in the fire. Like He brought his people out of Egypt."

Moriah held her breath, waiting to see how people reacted.

There was nothing, only blank, scared stares. Some members clung to each other. Some glanced around, looking desperate for a way to escape.

"If you agree with me, say 'amen.'" Gilead leaned toward the crowd in his normal charismatic manner. His words sounded persuasive. People wanted to believe him. He had an outstanding talent for getting people to do what he wanted. His face looked trust-worthy—but looks could be deceitful.

"Amen," a few people muttered.

"I can't hear you," Gilead prodded.

"Amen." It was a little louder this time.

"You're almost there."

"Amen," people finally said, their words strong. Some of their anxiety seemed to fade.

Not Moriah's.

"That's the spirit." Gilead paused. "Makirites, we are all here together bonded by our love of God and our calling to be better people. Let's repent together right now as we take the body and blood."

He held the bread up and instructed everyone to take it.

Then he raised the cup in his hands.

That was it, Moriah realized. That was Gilead's end game.

This wasn't just juice.

There was something else in that liquid.

It made sense.

This would be like one, big mass suicide. That's how it would look, at least.

"Now, let's raise our cups and take this communion together," Gilead continued.

Everyone raised their cups, imitating Gilead.

Moriah's heart raced.

She couldn't let everyone do this. They were all going to die for the Cause—only they didn't know it. And once they drank the juice, it would be too late.

Before she lost her courage, she stepped forward. "No!" Moriah yelled. "Everyone, stop!"

Gilead turned to her, fire in his eyes. "What are you doing, *dear*?"

She ignored him and turned toward the crowd. "Don't drink the juice. It's poisoned."

Another round of murmurs went around the compound.

"Don't be silly," Gilead said, his nostrils flaring "My wife hasn't been feeling well. Please, no one listen to her. She needs help."

"Listen to me! I'm not the crazy one. He is. He's going to kill you all!"

Dietrich came and took her arms, silently threatening Moriah harm if she spoke any more.

Her gaze veered toward movement in the distance. Several of Gilead's inner circle emerged from the kitchen, guns in their hands. They took positions at the windows. The boards that had once covered those windows had been moved, positioned several inches higher than normal to allow the gun barrels to protrude.

"I would never do that," Gilead assured everyone, even as sweat dotted his forehead. "Watch, I'll take the juice."

He swallowed the contents of his cup, which Moriah would bet wasn't poisoned like the rest.

"Besides, we all know where we're going," Gilead continued, giving an award-winning performance in front of his followers. "We're going to heaven. There's no fear in death. This juice isn't poisoned, but we shouldn't live in fear here on this earth. That's something I've been trying to teach you all."

Moriah watched as the crowds seemed to calm, buying into what Gilead was selling . . . again. No! Why wouldn't they listen to her?

At Gilead's prompting, they raised their cups again. Brought them to their lips.

And then more gunfire rang out.

———

CASSIDY DUCKED BEHIND A TREE AS MORE BULLETS whizzed past. The rain came down harder. Harder.

Thunder rumbled. Lightning lit the sky. The storm was fully upon them.

The situation had just turned even more hostile.

Whatever was happening in the Meeting Place, Gilead didn't want them to know about it.

"How many shooters do you see?" Fielding asked into the com.

"I see three more," Easton said.

"I see three also," Cassidy confirmed.

"Let's take them down," Fielding said. "We need to get inside that building. We don't have any time to waste."

Cassidy agreed.

Fielding barked out orders on who was to take on which shooter.

One by one, the men fell to the ground.

Cassidy waited a minute, hardly able to breathe as she waited to see what would unfold next.

There was nothing else. No more gunfire.

Had they really gotten all of the armed men surrounding the Meeting Place?

It seemed too easy.

"Let's move in," Fielding said. "Watch your backs. We don't know what we're up against right now."

Ignoring the rain that hammered her face, Cassidy moved forward, gripping her gun—a different one than her usual, since Gilead had taken her Glock.

She would do this for Ty. She'd do it for the residents inside. For the innocent people who'd been manipulated into this way of life.

No one would ever thrive unless they got out of this place and out from under Anthony Gilead's mind-controlling tactics.

Six feet from the building, a surge of hope went through Cassidy. Maybe this wouldn't be as bad as she thought.

Just as the thought fluttered through her mind, men appeared at the windows. Bullets began flying through the air, piercing the trees and ground around her.

Someone let out a groan beside her.

Cassidy swung her head toward the sound.

It was Easton.

Moving quickly, Cassidy knelt beside him on the muddy ground, scanning him for injuries. "Are you okay?"

He nodded, holding his leg with a grimace on his face. "I'll be fine. Go on."

"Are you sure?" She didn't want to leave him

here injured, yet she felt torn. Those people inside needed her help also.

Easton nodded again. "Yeah, I'm positive. Get these guys before everyone inside dies."

Dear Lord, please help us.

As more shots rang out, Cassidy dragged Easton behind a tree. She greedily sucked in deep breaths of air as her heart hammered in her chest.

Those men . . . they had automatic weapons.

What was her team going to do? How were they going to get through?

Cassidy peered out from behind the tree. There were four windows on this side of the building. Lights illuminated the inside of the Meeting Place, but she couldn't make out any details. All she could see were the silhouettes of the men with weapons crouched there.

"We may need to call in backup," Fielding said.

"It will be too late by then," Cassidy yelled over the roar of the storm.

"I'm inclined to agree with her," Abbott said. "Something is going down inside that building. There's no reason for these people to be meeting at this hour."

Cassidy strained to see what was happening in the building.

She heard yells. Screams.

Her heart leapt into her throat. This was a tragedy. A total tragedy—one that Cassidy felt powerless to stop.

Please, Lord. Help them also.

CHAPTER TWENTY-SIX

MORIAH WATCHED in horror as people put the cups to their lips.

Several hesitated, not throwing their heads back to take the juice. Others did as they were told and sipped the drink.

Moriah held her breath and waited to see what would happen.

No, no, no . . .

This was worse than she'd ever imagined. She could practically smell fear in the room, the same scent she'd experienced when she'd gone to a slaughterhouse with her father once.

Only these people weren't cattle. No, there were women in here. Children.

How could Gilead be this cruel?

"You can stop them," she whispered to Dietrich.

"No, I can't."

"Yes, you can," she whispered. "You're the only one."

As soon as Moriah said the words, she saw another man approach a family who'd refused to drink. He raised a gun toward them. The woman pulled her son closer, burying his face, as the father stepped in front of both of them.

"Drink the juice," the gunman ordered.

The father shook his head. "No."

"Drink the juice or I'll shoot. Do it! Now!"

The man's wife cried out beside him. Moriah braced herself for more violence, praying against it. Praying for safety for that little family.

Before she could see what happened, someone screamed across the room. Moriah jerked her head toward the sound. A man dropped onto the floor, his body going into convulsions. Another man knelt beside him.

"We need an ambulance!"

The gunmen perched at the windows continued to fire. Someone else ran toward the front doors and tried to get out. They couldn't.

The doors were locked.

The squall in the room continued to grow in intensity.

Even God himself seemed upset. Thunder

rumbled and lightning struck. She could hear the wind hitting the walls with enough force that the building rattled.

It felt like the end of the world was happening around her as evil ravaged this place.

"Dietrich, please," she whispered, glancing up at him. "Serena said she saw something decent inside you. She was right. Don't let evil win."

He stared out at the crowd and flinched. He didn't like this either, did he? He might not admit it, but he was having a crisis of conscience. She could see it on his face.

Then one of the gunmen walked up to Serena and placed a gun to her head.

"Drink it," he ordered.

Serena stared at the man for a minute before flipping her cup over and pouring the juice on the floor.

The man grabbed her am and pulled her toward the front.

He was going to make an example of her, wasn't he?

Dietrich bristled beside Moriah, his eyes fastened on the scene.

All the chaos around them faded, and all Moriah could see was her friend—maybe her only friend in this place—being led to the stage. She could sense an execution was about to play out.

Gilead watched with an evil gleam in his eyes. He poured Serena another cup of juice and held it to her lips.

"Drink, my child," he crooned. "Drink and be cleansed."

"I'm already cleansed, and it has nothing to do with you or your sacraments." Serena raised her chin.

Gilead's eyes darkened. "You don't know what you're talking about."

"I do."

Gilead nodded at one of his men—a big, burly giant named Enoch. The foot soldier trod over to Serena and pointed his gun at her.

"Show us your faith, Serena," Gilead said. "Show us how ready you are to face the afterlife."

Moriah tugged against Dietrich's grip, praying he might do something. That he'd have a change of heart.

Before it was too late.

But for now, everyone watched and waited.

What was Serena going to do?

———

CASSIDY HEARD MORE SCREAMS INSIDE. AND THEN SHE heard something even worse.

Silence.

She closed her eyes, just for a minute. Even from outside, she could feel the terror coming from inside those walls. She could sense the desperation of those captive there.

"There are more of these guys than we have people out here," Fielding said in his com. "Going inside right now would be a death mission."

"We can't just leave these people." Cassidy's gaze locked on the building as she prayed desperate prayers. "I see four more gunmen. We can take them."

"There are five by the windows," Fielding said. "But how many more inside? What are they going to do if we keep pressing in? They could turn the guns on their own."

"Their chances are still better if they do that than they are if we leave them on their own right now," Abbott said.

Fielding remained silent a moment.

"We just can't risk it, everyone," he finally said. "We need to wait for backup."

Frustration surged inside Cassidy. She knew why he'd said that, but she also knew that none of these people would survive if their team stayed out here.

"We have to move in," Cassidy said again. She couldn't stress that enough. Knowing what she did now about the poison . . . she visualized Jonestown playing out all over again.

The rain pelted her face, and thunder rumbled again.

The violent storm remained on top of them. The winds tossed the tops of trees back and forth. The rain fell unrelenting. The thunder sounded like it might crush them.

Lightning flashed over the trees. Then flashed again, accompanied by another loud crack of thunder.

As the sky lit with purple again, a bolt snaked across the sky, shattering it with streaks of electricity as far as the eye could see.

Thunder seemed to shake the ground, followed by a bright flash that nearly blinded her. Instinctively, she raised her hand over her face, trying to protect herself.

Screams sounded in the distance.

Cassidy jerked her eyes back open. Sparks rained down around her.

Lightning had hit something nearby, she realized.

Cassidy jerked her gaze around, trying to find the source.

Then she sucked in a breath.

The bolt had struck the roof of the Meeting Place.

Cassidy didn't know if this was an answer to prayer or a curse.

But she was going to assume this was their opportunity to move in. This was a life or death situation.

She charged toward the building.

CHAPTER TWENTY-SEVEN

MORIAH WATCHED as Gilead forced the cup to Serena's lips.

Her friend stood strong, her gaze firm, despite the moisture in her eyes.

Around them, more people fell to the floor. Others screamed. Some cried.

Gilead's men still held guns. Still paced. Still carried out orders.

"Dietrich," she whispered one more time.

He sucked in a breath, tense as he held her arm. His breaths came faster. Faster.

Suddenly, Dietrich shoved Moriah away with enough force that she hit the floor.

She raised her head in time to see Dietrich tackle the gunman.

The weapon fired.

Dietrich's hands went to his stomach. A red blotch appeared there, growing bigger by the moment.

Moriah gasped.

That was blood. Dietrich had been shot.

Her gaze flickered to Serena. Her friend let out a cry before reaching for him, holding his head in her lap as life began to slip away.

Gilead stepped back, as if unsure what to do. Everything was falling apart. He had to realize that.

A crack sounded directly on top of them. The lights went out. The smell of something burning filled the air.

And then the fire came.

Fire from above.

No, it was lightning, she realized. The building had been struck by lightning.

Instantly, flames consumed the ceiling. People panicked. Ran toward the doors, which were locked. They nearly trampled each other in their desperation to get out.

But they couldn't.

They were trapped in here. If the poison or gunmen didn't kill them, the fire would.

Her gaze went to Gilead. He took a step back. And back. And back.

He was trying to slip away from this chaos he'd created.

And he might succeed.

The ceiling still burned. The fire spread rapidly. Faster than Moriah expected with the rain.

Smoke filled the space.

A thud sounded against the doors. Then another one. And another one.

Someone was trying to break down the door from the outside.

Another thud, and the doors burst open. A SWAT team invaded the room, urging people outside and to safety.

One of the officers bypassed the crowds and darted to her, kneeling on the floor where she lay.

Realization flooded Moriah. It was Chief Chambers. She'd come over to Moriah to help her, even after everything Moriah had put her through.

"Gilead went that way," Moriah said, pointing to the back of the building. "I'll be fine. Go get him."

"You're sure?"

Moriah nodded. "More than sure."

Cassidy nodded and took off.

———

CASSIDY DODGED A TIMBER AS IT FELL FROM ABOVE,

crashing to the floor. This whole place was about to go up in flames. The wood here was so old that it made perfect kindling for hungry fire.

Fielding and his team tried to control the panicking crowds and escort them out. It didn't matter. They tramped toward the doors, frantic to escape.

Hopefully, the agents could get to the gunmen.

All Cassidy focused on was catching Gilead.

She stepped out the back door and into the rain just in time to see Gilead's fleeing figure.

She fired her gun in the air.

"Stop right there, Gilead, or I'll shoot you," she yelled.

To her surprise, Gilead stopped. He raised his hands in the air and slowly turned around.

Cassidy closed the space between them, her gun aimed at him.

"You didn't think you were going to get away that easily, did you?" she asked.

"Actually, I did." He smiled at her, almost looking impressed. "You're a smart woman, Cassidy Chambers. I underestimated you. Thought you were just a pretty face. Thought you got hired to be eye candy here on the island. Like they could have their own little version of *Baywatch*."

"That's all women are to you, isn't it?

Subservient. Meant for your pleasure. Meant to make your life easier."

"The Bible does say women were designed to be a helpmate."

"I think you need to read further. There are women in the Bible who did great things for God—things that didn't include cooking and cleaning."

"You're feisty. I like that."

Rain drizzled down Cassidy's face, but she didn't care. She wasn't going to let this man out of her sight. She could hear the fire burning behind her—roaring at times as it consumed the building. People screamed. Footsteps pounded. Her team members talked to each other in her com.

She ignored it all.

"Why did you do all of this, Gilead?" she asked. "Don't tell me because God told you to."

Gilead didn't say anything for a moment. Cassidy was sure he was going to make up another glib, arrogant excuse.

Instead, he said, "I just wanted to be somebody. There. You have the truth. Are you happy?"

No, she wasn't happy. Nothing about this situation made her happy. "You were going to kill all these people tonight just because you selfishly wanted to 'be somebody.'"

He raised his palms, unaffected by her words. "What can I say? We shouldn't be afraid of death."

"Nor should we force it upon other people."

He scowled and glanced behind her as more of the building collapsed. Cassidy could hear it happening, but she still didn't move. Didn't look.

No, all of her attention was on Gilead.

"I didn't want them to have to go through this," he said.

"Go through what?" Fire caused by lightning? The trauma of the siege around them? Being held at gunpoint by a homicidal maniac?

His eyes glazed. "All of this. I tried to make it easy for them. Tried to let them go to a happy place where all their troubles would be gone."

"Maybe that's not what they wanted for themselves."

He shrugged, his shoulders loosening and his words slurring together. "Life isn't all it's cracked up to be, is it?"

"Gilead?" She watched him. Watched his expression freeze. Watched his muscles loosen.

He'd taken the poison, she realized.

She sucked in a breath.

He wasn't getting out of this that easily.

"I need medical assistance," she said into her com.

Then she handcuffed Gilead, to make sure he wouldn't get away.

She hoped the paramedics would get here in time.

CHAPTER TWENTY-EIGHT

AN HOUR LATER, the rain had stopped, leaving a soppy mess around them.

The same storm that had started the fire had put the fire out. The Meeting Place was now just a skeleton, however. Its remains stood as a reminder of what happened when darkness was clothed as light.

Firefighters had arrived and extinguished any pop-up blazes that occurred. Paramedics treated victims. Other officers took statements.

So far, they'd found twenty bodies. Four were gunmen that had been shot by their team. Three people had died because of the fire. And the rest had drunk the poison.

Dietrich had taken a gunshot to the abdomen, but he was still hanging on. Abbott was with him as paramedics put him into the ambulance. Maybe—just maybe—Dietrich would turn his life around.

Abbott had muttered a soft "thank you" to Cassidy as they'd passed, and Cassidy had realized maybe he wasn't the enemy after all. He was just someone trying to protect a loved one. Maybe his methods weren't the best, but that didn't make him a bad guy.

Gilead was also being treated, and Cassidy hoped he lived to face the consequences of what he'd done. He needed to pay for all the harm he'd caused in these people's lives. Cassidy didn't know if that would mean life in prison or something more drastic. She would leave that to the courts to decide.

She glanced across the group of Gilead's Cove members. Many had blankets wrapped around them. EMTs from all over the Outer Banks had shown up to help.

It looked like a scene she would see in a wartime movie. Everyone just looked so, so . . . hopeless.

As she wove between the crowds, a familiar face came into view.

Serena.

Cassidy rushed between people, trying to reach her. As soon as she got close enough, Cassidy pulled the girl into an embrace. Serena broke down and bawled in Cassidy's arms.

"I should have never done this," Serena cried. "You were right, Cassidy."

"It's okay," Cassidy murmured, resting her chin on the woman's head as another tremble raked through Serena's body. "It's okay now."

Suddenly, Serena stiffened, and her eyes widened with urgency as she jerked out of Cassidy's arms. "How could I have forgotten? Ty . . . he's in a bunker. You've got to help him—"

"We found him," Cassidy said. "We found Ty. He's at the clinic being treated as we speak."

The air slowly released from her lungs. "You did?"

"We did. He should be okay."

Serena nearly crumpled in Cassidy's arms again. "I'm so glad to hear that. I was so scared for him. For me. For everyone."

"I know. We all were."

She sniffled and turned to look back at the remains of the Meeting Place. "Cassidy, when we were in there . . . Dietrich . . ."

"He was a bad man," Cassidy said. "I know."

Serena's red-rimmed eyes turned back to Cassidy, her gaze trying to communicate what words could only touch on. "No, you don't understand. Dietrich risked his life to save me. That man—Enoch—was about to put a bullet in my head, and Dietrich tackled him. He got shot in the process. Almost died."

Cassidy imagined the scene playing out. She supposed that everyone had a little good and a little evil inside them. Each person had to decide which side they should nurture and feed. At that moment, Dietrich had chosen to be selfless.

"I'm glad he redeemed himself," Cassidy said. "He obviously does care for you in his own way."

Serena stared off in the distance a moment before covering her face with her hands as another round of agony seemed to consume her, and her chest rose and fell rapidly. "I don't know what I'm going to do, Cassidy. I don't know how I'm going to get through this. I don't know how I can move on after going through what I have. After seeing what I've seen."

Cassidy put her arm around her shoulders. "I don't either. But you will. You'll get through this. We'll help you."

She sniffled again and leaned into Cassidy.

As they stood there, Moriah slowly approached them. Her stringy hair clung to her face. Dirt smudged her skin. She was barefoot.

But she was more alive than Cassidy had ever seen her. She had a new hope in her eyes, and this time it wasn't because of Gilead's empty promises. But the hope was lined with grief. A lot of grief.

"Chief, Ty is in a bunker—"

"We found him," Cassidy said. "Thank you, though."

"Good. I'm glad he's been rescued." She paused. "I could have stopped this." Moriah's voice stilled with sadness. "If I'd seen it in time."

"No one saw this coming," Cassidy told her. "Don't be too hard on yourself."

"I just wanted my happily ever after."

"You'll get it. Just be patient."

She wrapped her arms over her chest, moisture rimming her eyes. "What was in that juice?"

Cassidy shrugged. "I don't know. I have a feeling it was a mix of drugs. Your friend Ruth had a hand in developing them."

Moriah winced. "Ruth?"

"That's right. She worked for poison control. I guess she's always been fascinated with drug combinations and unusual poisons. In fact, one of my colleagues just told me there was a warrant out for her. She actually poisoned her husband."

"Ruth?" Moriah repeated.

Cassidy nodded. "Yes, Ruth."

"I had no idea." She ran her sleeve beneath her eyes. "Chief Chambers, I want to go home."

"I'm sure we can arrange something. But we're going to need to question you first. We need to know everything that happened here. That happened to you."

"If it means Anthony Gilead will be going to jail, I'd be happy to share everything I know." Moriah paused. "And Chief, you're real lucky to have someone like Ty in your life. I want to hold out for someone like him."

Yes, she was very blessed.

Cassidy's phone rang, and she saw that it was Doc Clemson. The doc? Did he have an update?

She pressed the phone to her ear, hardly able to breathe.

"Ty is awake, and he's asking for you," Clemson said.

Joy filled her heart. "I'll be right there."

———

CASSIDY RUSHED THROUGH THE CLINIC AND STOPPED outside of Ty's door to draw in a deep breath and attempt to compose herself.

She looked like a mess. Her hair was wet. Her police uniform was wet, muddy, and smelled like smoke. No doubt she had dirt on her. Maybe some soot.

She placed her hand on the doorknob when Doc Clemson called to her. "Cassidy."

She paused and turned. "Yes?"

"I figured out what he was poisoned with. It wasn't just salmonella. It was a mix of salmonella and some oleander."

"What?"

He nodded. "My guess is that these people were testing out several variations. I'm doing bloodwork on the Gilead's Cove members who've given permission. I have a feeling everyone there was given different mixes in their drinks. Gilead was trying to figure out the perfect combination to get the results he wanted."

"That's chilling, to say the least."

"Yes, it is." He squeezed her arm. "Good job out there tonight."

She smiled. "Thanks."

Wasting no more time, Cassidy turned the handle and stepped into her husband's room. Her eyes filled with warmth when she saw Ty sitting up in bed. She rushed toward him and buried herself in his chest, suddenly not caring how she looked.

"Oh, Ty." It felt so good to feel him beside her. Alive. Heart beating. Safe.

"Cassidy . . ."

She lifted her head, studying his eyes. They were still the same beautiful ocean-blue eyes as ever. That hadn't changed, even if his face was bruised and swollen.

"I've never been so happy to see you." Her voice cracked with emotion.

"Yeah, I know the feeling. I . . . I wasn't sure I was going to make it."

She rested her hand on the side of his face. "Neither were we. I don't think I've ever prayed so hard in my entire life. Everyone here on the island was praying."

"I felt those prayers, so thank you." Ty took her hand and gazed into her eyes. "Is it over?"

She sucked back a sob of joy and nodded. "Yeah, it is."

He smiled. "That's my girl."

"It was a hard fight."

"I know it was."

"But I think the island can finally rest."

"I think we all need a little rest, don't we?"

"Yes, we do." Cassidy leaned closer and gently pressed a kiss on her husband's lips. "I love you, Ty Chambers."

"I love you too, Cassidy. Always."

CHAPTER TWENTY-NINE

CASSIDY SAT on the swing that dangled from the ceiling of the screened-in porch at her cottage, Ty beside her. He'd come home from the clinic three days ago.

Home . . . what a beautiful word. A smile played across her face at the thought.

Home was this place where she held coffee in one hand and Ty's hand in the other. Where Kujo chased birds on the beach as the sun rose above the ocean in the distance. Where a new day promised new hope.

It had been a week since everything with Gilead's Cove went down, and the case against Anthony Gilead would be building for quite a while. The good news was that a lot of the members who'd been a part of his movement were now getting the help they needed. Just as Doc Clemson had suspected, many of them had ingested poison throughout their stay at Gilead's Cove. It was like Gilead's followers were also lab rats for him.

Including Moriah.

She'd been questioned and had then gone to stay with her parents in West Virginia until she could figure the future out. She'd promised to stay in touch. She would also be one of the key witnesses at Gilead's trial.

Dietrich was in jail again, but maybe he'd learned his lesson this time. At least he'd redeemed himself.

Ruth was also in prison, facing some pretty serious charges for her involvement in creating the poison.

Gilead's Cove had been officially closed and locks had been put over the gate there. It was like a cemetery, this one memorializing death instead of life.

Cassidy didn't think anyone here on the island would forget about what went down there any time soon.

For the first time in many years, it appeared Rhonda Becker might actually be able to build a new life for herself, no longer fearing her ex-husband finding her. She'd left the island a few days ago with tears of joy streaming down her face.

Since the FBI had taken over the investigation, they were representing the situation to the media. Cassidy could keep her face off the news.

But that didn't change the fact that Gilead knew who she really was. And that he was still alive and still holding it over her head. A small part of her realized that, if the man had died—if Cassidy hadn't gotten him help—then her secret would have died with him. But it wasn't Cassidy's job to choose who lived or died.

She pushed down her thoughts and squeezed Ty's hand again. She wouldn't think about that now. Right now, she would think about all she had to be grateful for.

Ty was home. He was a little worse for wear, but he would be fine. His arm was in a sling, and his ribs were wrapped. But he was 100 percent better today than he'd been last week at the same time.

"So, Mac is our new mayor . . ." Ty said. The election had taken place yesterday, and Mac had won by a wide margin.

"Thank goodness. No one deserves it more."

"I agree."

She leaned back. "You know, in some ways, everything that happened seems like a nightmare. It doesn't seem real."

"I agree. The whole situation with Gilead's Cove just goes to prove the saying that evil prevails when good people do nothing. Just think what would have happened if you didn't step in."

"I wish I felt like a hero. But people still died that night."

"Not as many as would have died if you hadn't been there." He squeezed her hand. "You're my hero, Cassidy. I'm so glad to be back home with you."

"I'm so glad to have you home with me." Cassidy leaned her head on his shoulder, remembering those moments when she'd thought she'd lost him. "I was so scared, Ty."

"I know. But everything's okay right now. We just have to be thankful for that."

"Yes, we do," Cassidy said.

Ty shifted, lifting his head to the breeze that swept across the dune. "So how about Wes and Paige?"

"Are they dating?" Cassidy asked. Paige had officially come on staff at the station, and she'd been doing a great job so far. She'd noticed Wes was coming by the office a lot more.

"I don't think anything is official, but I've never seen Wes look so smitten. He's definitely interested."

"It will be interesting to see what happens then."

"Yes, it will be. We just need to get Austin and Skye a wedding date, make sure Wes doesn't blow things with Paige, and our whole crew will have gone from single to happily coupled."

Cassidy smiled at the thought. She wanted all her friends to be as happy as she was. She was glad that appeared to be the case.

"Oh, by the way, my mom called last night," Ty said.

"Is she okay?" She'd been going through some treatments for cancer.

"She's fine. She actually called to tell me that . . ."

Cassidy turned toward him, worry rushing through her. "What is it?"

"That she and Dad have bought the cottage next door."

Cassidy's eyes widened, and she wasn't certain if she'd heard him correctly. "What?"

He nodded slowly, as if unsure what Cassidy's reaction might be. "Yeah, she wanted to surprise us."

"Well, that's surprising all right. That's . . . great."

"They thought the slower pace here would be good for them as Mom recovers."

"It will be nice to have them close," Cassidy said. She liked his parents. She really did. And though she might not have chosen the location right next door for their permanent residence, she would gladly welcome them into her life here on Lantern Beach.

"Thanks for being a good sport." Ty glanced down at her. "Speaking of family, what's going on with your dad?"

She shrugged and took another sip of her coffee. "He's actually recovering well from his stroke. Despite the doctor's original prognosis, they think he might be able to take the reins at the company again."

"That's good news."

"It is. My mom didn't tell me that." Cassidy frowned. "She's still not happy with me for not returning home to take over the company. But I read an article online about him. There were even pictures. It was . . . well, it was good to see an update. I know my mom was worried, and I regretted that I couldn't help."

"I'm glad it worked out."

A few minutes of silence passed as they swung back and forth.

"You're worried that Gilead will release information on you, aren't you?" Ty finally asked.

She licked her lips. "I am. I mean, I've built a life here. If he tells the wrong person . . ."

"Let's pray that doesn't happen."

As Ty said the words, Cassidy's phone rang. She glanced at the number and squinted.

"Who is it?" Ty asked.

"It's Arianna Stark, that reporter with the *Raleigh Times* who did the exposé on Anthony Gilead."

"Why would she be calling?"

"I have no idea." She frowned before letting out a sigh. "Let me answer. One minute."

She stood and paced away from Ty. "Hello, Arianna."

"Chief Chambers, I hope I'm not calling too early."

"Not at all. What can I do for you?"

"Listen, I just wanted to come right to you with something that Anthony Gilead is trying to pull."

She braced herself, wondering what the man could possibly be up to now. "What's that?"

"He's claiming you're Cady Matthews," Arianna blurted.

Cassidy swallowed hard, determined to keep her voice level. "Cady Matthews? Who is she?"

"You know . . . Commotio Cordis."

Cassidy said nothing, unwilling to show any recognition.

"She's that detective from Seattle who went undercover and killed Raul Sanders, the leader of that gang. She died about nine or ten months ago."

"But you said Anthony Gilead is claiming that I'm Cady Matthews?"

"I know. Crazy, isn't it?"

She stared out over the beach, hoping this wouldn't signal the end for her here. Ty's parents were moving here. She didn't want to have to pack up and leave now.

Or ever.

"Anyway, I wanted to let you know he was saying that. I actually looked up her picture, just out of curiosity."

"And?" Cassidy held her breath.

"The two of you have some similarities in build, but you're clearly not the same person. Even your eyes are different. They're bright with hope. Your skin is glowing. Even your smile is different. The man is clearly delusional."

"I think we all know that he's delusional."

"I know this is going to sound crazy, but I did a little digging."

Cassidy tensed again. "Did you?"

"I mean, that would be the story of my life. But the medical examiner's report . . . it clearly showed that Cady Matthews was dead. I looked online and found some old articles from when you were in high school out in Texas. In fact, forgive me, but I called your parents."

"My parents?" Cassidy glanced over at Ty.

His eyes widened with concern.

"Yeah, I managed to track them down. They retired in Florida, huh? Anyway, your dad said my idea was crazy. He talked about your days in the rodeo, about when you lost one of your baby teeth while singing with the children's choir at church. He sounds like a great guy."

Cassidy closed her eyes as she listened. Samuel Stephens, her contact with the FBI and the man who'd helped her disappear permanently, must have taken that call. He'd done a great job creating a new life for her.

"My dad is a great guy. Anyway, I appreciate you letting me know what Anthony Gilead is up to."

"Of course. I just don't want to see him destroy any other innocent lives with his lies, you know?"

"Yeah, I know. Thank you again."

Cassidy ended the call and passed on the information to Ty. He rose to his feet, met her there in the middle of the porch, and placed a tender kiss on her forehead. "Good. I'm glad. That's what every reporter is going to think. No one will give him any attention."

"I hope so."

They turned as steps clunked up the stairs. Cassidy tensed, halfway expecting more trouble.

Instead, Colton Locke appeared.

Cassidy and Ty stepped back from each other.

"Hope I'm not interrupting anything," Colton said, amusement dancing in his eyes. He was staying at one of the cabanas behind their cottage and had been a regular fixture around here for the past week.

"Not at all," Ty said. "What's going on?"

"I have something I'd like to go over with you. It's pertaining to the new offshoot of Hope House that we talked about starting. I've been brainstorming some ideas."

"I'd love to hear them," Ty said.

"I'll save the boring details for later," he said. "But I did come up with a name."

"What have you got?" Cassidy asked. She thought this whole idea was great. There was obviously a need for services like what they could offer. Cassidy wouldn't have found Ty if it hadn't been for the help and expertise of Colton and his friends.

"Blackout," Colton said. "I thought it fit since the work we'll be doing is off the books."

Ty nodded slowly. "I like it."

"I have more details I can discuss with you later. I just wanted to run that name past you. I kind of like it. A lot," Colton added with a grin.

"Let's definitely meet a little later. I want to hear more."

Colton nodded and winked. "Sounds good. Okay, I'll catch you two later. Get back to enjoying your morning together."

As he walked away, Ty and Cassidy sat back on the swing. Ty took Cassidy's hand in his. And in a comfortable quiet, they watched the water, and relished the simple moments together.

COMING NEXT: LANTERN BEACH BLACKOUT

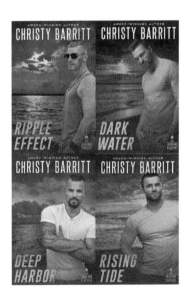

Four former Navy SEALs with a dark secret must confront their pasts in order to move forward.

AND DON'T MISS: WINDS OF DANGER

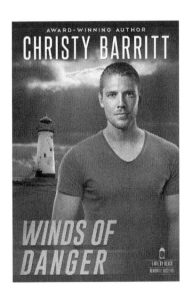

Coming late summer/early fall: Wes's story!

ALSO BY CHRISTY BARRITT:

OTHER BOOKS IN THE LANTERN BEACH SERIES:

LANTERN BEACH MYSTERIES

Hidden Currents

You can take the detective out of the investigation, but you can't take the investigator out of the detective. A notorious gang puts a bounty on Detective Cady Matthews's head after she takes down their leader, leaving her no choice but to hide until she can testify at trial. But her temporary home across the country on a remote North Carolina island isn't as peaceful as she initially thinks. Living under the new identity of Cassidy Livingston, she struggles to keep her investigative skills tucked away, especially after a body washes ashore. When local police bungle the murder investigation, she can't resist stepping in. But Cassidy is supposed to be keeping a low profile. One wrong move could lead to both her discovery and her demise. Can she bring justice to the island . . . or will the hidden currents surrounding her pull her under for good?

Flood Watch

The tide is high, and so is the danger on Lantern Beach. Still in hiding after infiltrating a dangerous gang, Cassidy Livingston just has to make it a few more months before she can testify at trial and resume her old life. But trouble keeps finding her, and Cassidy is pulled into a local investigation after a man mysteriously disappears from the island she now calls home. A recurring nightmare from her time undercover only muddies things, as does a visit from the parents of her handsome ex-Navy SEAL neighbor. When a friend's life is threatened, Cassidy must make choices that put her on the verge of blowing her cover. With a flood watch on her emotions and her life in a tangle, will Cassidy find the truth? Or will her past finally drown her?

Storm Surge

A storm is brewing hundreds of miles away, but its effects are devastating even from afar. Laid-back, loose, and light: that's Cassidy Livingston's new motto. But when a makeshift boat with a bloody cloth inside washes ashore near her oceanfront home, her detective instincts shift into gear . . . again. Seeking clues isn't the only thing on her mind—romance is heating up with next-door neighbor and former Navy SEAL Ty Chambers as well. Her heart wants the love and stability she's longed for her entire life. But her hidden identity only leads to a tidal wave of turbulence. As more answers emerge about the boat, the danger around her rises, creating a treacherous swell that threatens to reveal her past. Can Cassidy mind her own business, or will the storm surge of violence and corruption that has washed ashore on Lantern Beach leave her life in wreckage?

Dangerous Waters

Danger lurks on the horizon, leaving only two choices: find shelter or flee. Cassidy Livingston's new identity has begun to feel as comfortable as her favorite sweater. She's been tucked away on Lantern Beach for weeks, waiting to testify against a deadly gang, and is settling in to a new life she wants to last forever. When she thinks she spots someone malevolent from her past, panic swells inside her. If an enemy has found her, Cassidy won't be the only one who's a target. Everyone she's come to love will also be at risk. Dangerous waters threaten to pull her into an overpowering chasm she may never escape. Can

Cassidy survive what lies ahead? Or has the tide fatally turned against her?

Perilous Riptide

Just when the current seems safer, an unseen danger emerges and threatens to destroy everything. When Cassidy Livingston finds a journal hidden deep in the recesses of her ice cream truck, her curiosity kicks into high gear. Islanders suspect that Elsa, the journal's owner, didn't die accidentally. Her final entry indicates their suspicions might be correct and that what Elsa observed on her final night may have led to her demise. Against the advice of Ty Chambers, her former Navy SEAL boyfriend, Cassidy taps into her detective skills and hunts for answers. But her search only leads to a skeletal body and trouble for both of them. As helplessness threatens to drown her, Cassidy is desperate to turn back time. Can Cassidy find what she needs to navigate the perilous situation? Or will the riptide surrounding her threaten everyone and everything Cassidy loves?

Deadly Undertow

The current's fatal pull is powerful, but so is one detective's will to live. When someone from Cassidy Livingston's past shows up on Lantern Beach and warns her of impending peril, opposing currents collide, threatening to drag her under. Running would be easy. But leaving would break her heart. Cassidy must decipher between the truth and lies, between reality and deception. Even more importantly, she must decide whom to trust and whom to fear. Her life depends on it. As danger rises and answers surface, everything Cassidy thought she knew is tested. In order to survive, Cassidy must take drastic measures and end the battle against the ruthless gang DH-7 once and for all. But if her final mission fails, the consequences will be as deadly as the raging undertow.

LANTERN BEACH ROMANTIC SUSPENSE

Tides of Deception

Change has come to Lantern Beach: a new police chief, a new season, and . . . a new romance? Austin Brooks has loved Skye Lavinia from the moment they met, but the walls she keeps around her seem impenetrable. Skye knows Austin is the best thing to ever happen to her. Yet she also knows that if he learns the truth about her past, he'd be a fool not to run. A chance encounter brings secrets bubbling to the surface, and danger soon follows. Are the life-threatening events plaguing them really accidents . . . or is someone trying to send a deadly message? With the tides on Lantern Beach come deception and lies. One question remains—who will be swept away as the water shifts? And will it bring the end for Austin and Skye, or merely the beginning?

Shadow of Intrigue

For her entire life, Lisa Garth has felt like a supporting character in the drama of life. The designation never bothered her—until now. Lantern Beach, where she's settled and runs a popular restaurant, has boarded up for the season. The slower pace leaves her with too much time alone. Braden Dillinger came to Lantern Beach to try to heal. The former Special Forces officer returned from battle with invisible scars and diminished hope. But his recovery is hampered by the fact that an unknown enemy is trying to kill him. From the moment Lisa and Braden meet, danger ignites around them, and both are drawn into a web of intrigue that turns their lives upside down. As shadows creep in, will Lisa and Braden be able to shine a light on the peril around them? Or will the encroaching darkness turn their worst nightmares into reality?

Storm of Doubt

A pastor who's lost faith in God. A romance

writer who's lost faith in love. A faceless man with a deadly obsession. Nothing has felt right in Pastor Jack Wilson's world since his wife died two years ago. He hoped coming to Lantern Beach might help soothe the ragged edges of his soul. Instead, he feels more alone than ever. Novelist Juliette Grace came to the island to hide away. Though her professional life has never been better, her personal life has imploded. Her husband left her and a stalker's threats have grown more and more dangerous. When Jack saves Juliette from an attack, he sees the terror in her gaze and knows he must protect her. But when danger strikes again, will Jack be able to keep her safe? Or will the approaching storm prove too strong to withstand?

LANTERN BEACH PD

On the Lookout

When Cassidy Chambers accepted the job as police chief on Lantern Beach, she knew the island had its secrets. But a suspicious death with potentially far-reaching implications will test all her skills —and threaten to reveal her true identity. Cassidy enlists the help of her husband, former Navy SEAL Ty Chambers. As they dig for answers, both uncover parts of their pasts that are best left buried. Not everything is as it seems, and they must figure out if their John Doe is connected to the secretive group that has moved onto the island. As facts materialize, danger on the island grows. Can Cassidy and Ty discover the truth about the shadowy crimes in their cozy community? Or has darkness permanently invaded their beloved Lantern Beach?

Attempt to Locate

A fun girls' night out turns into a nightmare when armed robbers barge into the store where Cassidy and her friends are shopping. As the situation escalates and the men escape, a massive manhunt launches on Lantern Beach to apprehend the dangerous trio. In the midst of the chaos, a potential foe asks for Cassidy's help. He needs to find his sister who fled from the secretive Gilead's Cove community on the island. But the more Cassidy learns about the seemingly untouchable group, the more her unease grows. The pressure to solve both cases continues to mount. But as the gravity of the situation rises, so does the danger. Cassidy is determined to protect the island and break up the cult . . . but doing so might cost her everything.

First Degree Murder

Police Chief Cassidy Chambers longs for a break

from the recent crimes plaguing Lantern Beach. She simply wants to enjoy her friends' upcoming wedding, to prepare for the busy tourist season about to slam the island, and to gather all the dirt she can on the suspicious community that's invaded the town. But trouble explodes on the island, sending residents—including Cassidy—into a squall of uneasiness. Cassidy may have more than one enemy plotting her demise, and the collateral damage seems unthinkable. As the temperature rises, so does the pressure to find answers. Someone is determined that Lantern Beach would be better off without their new police chief. And for Cassidy, one wrong move could mean certain death.

Dead on Arrival

With a highly charged local election consuming the community, Police Chief Cassidy Chambers braces herself for a challenging day of breaking up petty conflicts and tamping down high emotions. But when widespread food poisoning spreads among potential voters across the island, Cassidy smells something rotten in the air. As Cassidy examines every possibility to uncover what's going on, local enigma Anthony Gilead again comes on her radar. The man is running for mayor and his cult-like following is growing at an alarming rate. Cassidy feels certain he has a spy embedded in her inner circle. The problem is that her pool of suspects gets deeper every day. Can Cassidy get to the bottom of what's eating away at her peaceful island home? Will voters turn out despite the outbreak of illness plaguing their tranquil town? And the even bigger question: Has darkness come to stay on Lantern Beach?

On her way to completing a degree in forensic science, Gabby St. Claire drops out of school and starts her own crime-scene cleaning business. When a routine cleaning job uncovers a murder weapon the police overlooked, she realizes that the wrong person is in jail. She also realizes that crime scene cleaning might be the perfect career for utilizing her investigative skills.

#1 Hazardous Duty
#2 Suspicious Minds
#2.5 It Came Upon a Midnight Crime (novella)
#3 Organized Grime
#4 Dirty Deeds
#5 The Scum of All Fears
#6 To Love, Honor and Perish

THE WORST DETECTIVE EVER:

I'm not really a private detective. I just play one on TV.

Joey Darling, better known to the world as Raven Remington, detective extraordinaire, is trying to separate herself from her invincible alter ego. She played the spunky character for five years on the hit TV show *Relentless*, which catapulted her to fame and into the role of Hollywood's sweetheart. When her marriage falls apart, her finances dwindle to nothing, and her father disappears, Joey finds herself on the Outer Banks of North Carolina, trying to piece together her life away from the limelight. But as people continually mistake her for the character she played on TV, she's tasked with solving real life crimes . . . even though she's terrible at it.

ABOUT THE AUTHOR

USA Today has called Christy Barritt's books "scary, funny, passionate, and quirky."

Christy writes both mystery and romantic suspense novels that are clean with underlying messages of faith. Her books have won the Daphne du Maurier Award for Excellence in Suspense and Mystery, have been twice nominated for the Romantic Times Reviewers' Choice Award, and have finaled for both a Carol Award and Foreword Magazine's Book of the Year.

She is married to her Prince Charming, a man who thinks she's hilarious—but only when she's not trying to be. Christy is a self-proclaimed klutz, an avid music lover who's known for spontaneously bursting into song, and a road trip aficionado.

When she's not working or spending time with her family, she enjoys singing, playing the guitar, and exploring small, unsuspecting towns where people have no idea how accident-prone she is.

Find Christy online at:
www.christybarritt.com
www.facebook.com/christybarritt
www.twitter.com/cbarritt

Sign up for Christy's newsletter to get information on all of her latest releases here: **www.christybarritt. com/newsletter-sign-up/**

If you enjoyed this book, please consider leaving a review.

Made in the USA
Columbia, SC
26 June 2019